ZONA GALE

Miss Lulu Bett

Born in Portage, Wisconsin, in 1874, Zona Gale graduated from the University of Wisconsin and first worked as a reporter in Milwaukee and New York City. She achieved a national reputation as a short-story writer in the booming magazine market of the early twentieth century. Author of eight novels, including *Birth* (1918) and *Faint Perfume* (1923) and collections of short stories as well as plays and poetry, Gale achieved her greatest critical and commercial success with *Miss Lulu Bett*, published in 1920. She also became an eminent social activist and essayist for progressive causes. She died in Chicago in 1938.

Barbara H. Solomon is a professor of English and Women's Studies at Iona College. Among the books she has edited are *The Awakening and Selected Stories of Kate Chopin*, *Herland and Selected Stories* by Charlotte Perkins Gilman, and *Once Upon a Childhood: Stories and Memoirs of American Youth* (with Eileen Panetta). She lives in New Rochelle, New York.

Eileen Panetta is an associate professor of English at Iona College. She is the coeditor of *Once Upon a Childhood* (with Barbara H. Solomon). She lives in New York City.

MISS LULU BETT

and Stories

MISS LULU BETT

and Stories

ZONA GALE

Edited by Barbara H. Solomon and Eileen Panetta

ANCHOR BOOKS
A DIVISION OF RANDOM HOUSE, INC.
NEW YORK

AN ANCHOR BOOKS ORIGINAL, DECEMBER 2005

Grateful acknowledgment is made to Leslyn Breese Keie for permission to
reprint the following: "The Need" and "Bridal Pond," originally published in
Bridal Pond (1930), and "The Biography of Blade," originally published in *Yellow
Gentians and Blue* (1927). Reprinted by permission of Leslyn Breese Keie.

Library of Congress Cataloging-in-Publication Data
Gale, Zona, 1874–1938.
Miss Lulu Bett and selected stories / Zona Gale ;
edited by Barbara H. Solomon and Eileen Panetta.
p. cm.
1. Miss Lulu Bett—Dream—The biography of Blade—The need—Bridal pond.
2. Single women—Fiction. 3. Housekeepers—Fiction. 4. Divorced women—
Fiction. 5. Self-realization—Fiction. 6. Middle West—Fiction.
7. Feminist fiction. I. Title.
PS3513.A34 A6 2005
813'.52—dc22
2005048192

Vintage ISBN-10: 1-4000-9538-7
Vintage ISBN-13: 978-1-4000-9538-4

Author photograph © Wisconsin Historical Society
Book design by Debbie Glasserman

www.anchorbooks.com

Printed in the United States of America
10 9 8 7 6 5 4 3 2 1

CONTENTS

INTRODUCTION

Miss Lulu Bett

When Zona Gale published *Miss Lulu Bett*, her seventh novel, in February 1920 she must have been delighted—but also astounded—by the enormous popularity it quickly achieved and the critical acclaim with which it was almost universally greeted.

She was well-known as a short-story writer who sympathetically observed small-town life, and her previous novel *Birth* (1918), a realistic tale about a Midwestern man whose virtues fail to make him a success, was widely praised. But the response to this novel was of a different order. Heywood Broun of *The New York Times* proclaimed that "of all American novels received in the last six months, Zona Gale's *Miss Lulu Bett* seems at the top of the list." It became one of the two bestselling novels of the year, and less than a year later, Gale was persuaded to write a play based on the novel. Also called *Miss Lulu Bett*, it won the 1921 Pulitzer Prize for drama, the first awarded to a woman playwright.

Lulu Bett is unmarried and lives with her sister's family in the Midwestern town of Warbleton. The power in the family—the word "power" often appears in the novel—rests entirely with her prosperous brother-in-law, Dwight Deacon, who is a dentist and a justice of the peace. He affects a jocular air, but his jests are usually at someone else's expense. His wife, Ina, Lulu's sister, presides more gently, but her role does not extend much beyond exclaiming at events, reinforcing her husband's edicts, and communicating the comings and goings of her family, which includes her quarrelsome mother as well as daughters Di and Monona. Ina's role is an expansive one, however, by contrast with Lulu's.

The family has maintained the fiction that Lulu, in her mid-thirties, is too weak to work. Yet she's the house beast of burden (as the novel itself refers to her), the cook and housekeeper whose purchase of tulips for the dinner table her brother-in-law considers an inappropriate expense for someone in her position. This woman without alternatives suddenly discovers one in a rare family visit from a cosmopolitan, much-traveled brother-in-law. Lulu is too guileless to see Ninian Deacon as an opportunity—but his presence provokes a challenging wit in her, and an identity of which she has largely been unaware.

Gale deftly evokes Lulu's initial unease as she joins the family and their guest in the parlor. Sitting in a rocking chair in her starched white skirt, "Her lace front wrinkled when she sat, and perpetually she adjusted it. She curled her feet sidewise beneath her chair, her long wrists and veined hands lay along her lap in no relation to her." As awkward as Lulu feels, she resists the passivity that has been her pattern. When Ninian bluntly asks whether she is a Miss or a Mrs., she quietly tells him, then asks, "Which kind of a Mr. are you?" He is delighted and taken aback by her response: the inconsistency of the titles has never occurred to him, a point that feminists would continue to make for decades.

If power is one theme in *Miss Lulu Bett*, marriage is another—the dialogue and the characters' thoughts keep returning to it. In one of the novel's major turning points, during a Deacon family theater outing Ninian playfully proposes marriage to her, and Lulu, not to be outdone, accepts. What begins as a joke turns out surprisingly to the Deacons and the couple to have legitimacy as a wedding ceremony. Dwight thinks only of how to undo the results of the jest, and Ina is scandalized, but the next day Lulu and Ninian boldly set off on their honeymoon. The marriage quickly reveals an underside, however, and Lulu returns to Warbleton and her family. But she has tasted what it is to think and act for herself, and will no longer support a facade of family propriety at her own expense.

Gale weaves a parallel romance through the novel, that of Lulu's teenage niece Di, who is if anything more discontented with the family's prosaic life than Lulu is. When Di also takes flight with her teenage suitor, Gale wryly leaves it to Lulu, who has returned from her own impetuous marriage, to rescue Di. Lulu doesn't hesitate to track down Di and bring her home, and in the end Lulu's fearlessness does not fail her or her niece.

Gale's portrait of Lulu Bett is in a tradition of women writers who wrote sympathetically about unmarried women, as Rose Terry Cooke did in her story "How Celia Changed Her Mind" and Sarah Orne Jewett did in "Miss Peck's Promotion." (Yet Lulu's assertion of independence and her ability to elude punishment for it were unusual in the contemporary portrayal of women in fiction, married or not.) Lulu is untroubled by her failed marriage, even though her brother-in-law dreads a family scandal, and by the end of the novel she has a new suitor and new prospects for happiness.

There were other reasons for the novel's popularity beyond its depiction of the birth of a strong woman. *Miss Lulu Bett* topped the 1920 bestseller list along with Sinclair Lewis's *Main Street*. It was often observed that both novels were unrelievedly satirical portraits of small-town life. In his 1940 book *The American Novel 1789–1939*, the critic Carl Van Doren called the recoil from provincialism in these novels and works by Sherwood Anderson and Edgar Lee Masters "the revolt from the village." With an enthusiasm that betrays a fatigue with fictional celebrations of small-town virtue, Constance Rourke, in her review of *Miss Lulu Bett* in *The New Republic,* observed that the Deacons are "ruthlessly drawn; and at every turn they are made to betray the looseness of fiber, the tedious facility of thought and space and action . . . which characterize much of our native provincial life." She calls Lulu a "luminous spirit" without the sentimentality that characterizes so much of the literature that preceded her, including Gale's own. Rourke concludes that "the book stands as a signal accomplishment in American letters. . . . If a single storyteller can pass from the empty slipshod formalism which marked so much American narrative into something deep-cutting like *Miss Lulu Bett*, there may be a chance that our narrative art will emerge into a firmer growth." Readers were ready for more realism in their regional literature.

Several critics also called attention to Gale's ear for ordinary speech. In his admiring review in *The New York World*, Robert C. Benchley admitted coming to the book well after many publications had called it "great." Though he objected to the novel's happy ending, for him "the telling is almost incomparable.

Where Miss Gale excels is in her almost phonographic reproduction of the vocal process of the average American in a state of domesticity." He saw the novel as an answer to his complaint that "no American seems able to write down the futile, silly things that real people do and the terrible things they say," and he quotes at length from the dialogue. There was a familiarity to these conversations—and a humor in hearing them this way—that readers were not yet accustomed to finding in novels.

The novel's quick-paced plot has some of the headlong quality of Lulu's defection from her family. Though there is never any doubt whose side Gale is on—the narrator's satirical asides come thick and fast, and the characters other than Lulu have something of the quality of comic stereotypes—the author is not entirely unsympathetic to the other Deacons. She is just more interested in the social ramifications of a woman learning to assert her own desires.

In its defense of women, its quick and sure style, its humor and its gift for ordinary conversation, *Miss Lulu Bett* marked a passage in American literature and brought Zona Gale her greatest success. In a high-spirited way, it also rehearsed some of the themes that would spur Gale on to a remarkable career as a social activist.

Four Stories

Zona Gale first achieved a national reputation as a short-story writer. Altogether she published more than three hundred stories in the booming magazine market of the day, frequently appearing in magazines such as *The Delineator*, *The Outlook*, *Harper's Monthly*, *The American*, *Everybody's Magazine*, *The Atlantic Monthly*, *Woman's Home Companion*, and *Lippincott's Magazine*.

"Dream" (1919), the first story in this collection, is set in the mythical Midwestern community of Friendship Village, based on Gale's hometown of Portage, Wisconsin. The locus of most of Gale's stories, Friendship Village was in its time as recognizable an icon of small-town America as Winesburg, Ohio, and Gopher Prairie were to become. In all of the Friendship Village stories, Calliope Marsh is the first-person narrator and central character. An independent, unmarried woman, she is a wise and vigorous community leader who often functions as the spokesperson for Gale's progressive social and political views. Sometimes a little too predictably, she is the lone voice of reason, the conscience of the community. Calliope, who lacks the stature or authority of the town's businessmen and officials, often must use her wit and good sense to resolve problems caused by the status-conscious and narrow-minded, not infrequently the male leaders of the village. Beholden to no one, she is accustomed to speaking her mind, even when frankness is inconvenient.

Over the years, the stories bespoke a vision of civic-mindedness, of the forging through common exertions of an ever-improving community, a vision of American life as Gale was convinced it ought to be lived. Calliope's accomplices in these efforts are regularly, though not exclusively, her fellow townswomen, who want only her insight to do the right thing. At the heart of their endeavors is the wonderfully named Friendship Married Ladies' Cemetery Improvement Sodality, whose efforts extend beyond grave beautification to the general good.

To those reviewers familiar with the stories' earnest intentions, the satire evident in *Miss Lulu Bett* came as something of a surprise. But notes of disillusion had already begun to appear in some of the Friendship Village stories. In the fifth and last collection, published as *Peace in Friendship Village* (1919), Calliope becomes somewhat tougher and more down-to-earth. Nowhere is this change more apparent than in "Dream," a short story in which Calliope's good heart and sound instincts are pitted against an intolerant community.

The story begins with the arrival of newcomers to the neighborhood, a family whose good furniture, exotic name, and ability to afford a twenty-dollar rent promises a "'distinct addition to Friendship Village society'" according to Mis' Sykes, who is to be their next-door neighbor. She is determined, without having met or even seen them, to enlist the entire village in a reception surprise at the new family's home. Her plans are, of course, as much about positioning herself at the forefront of an advantageous connection as about welcoming the newcomers, and part of the pleasure of the story is that the reader can sense their potential for backfiring even before knowing how it will occur.

While the reception is still being planned, impulsive Calliope pays a visit to the Burton Fernandez house and discovers that the family, though exceptionally accomplished—the daughter is studying at Chicago University, and the son has won a war medal—is of African descent. Calliope ruefully recognizes that there is work to do if a humiliating social disaster is to be averted at the reception.

This story is distinguished from Gale's earlier ones by her clear-eyed acknowledgment of the distance between what the villagers ideally might be and their actual capacity for change. She has taken the measure of the race problem in the country and knows that not even a Calliope Marsh can prevail against it.

The story was originally called "The Reception Surprise" and dates from 1915, well before the existence of an established body of literature that dealt openly with racism. Although Gale submitted it to a number of magazine editors who had been regularly accepting her work, no one was willing to risk publishing it. In his rejection, one editor wrote that it might "harden a lot of people against the gradual trend of the Negroes into a better social position." Gale revised and retitled the story "Dream," which appeared in print for the first time in *Peace in Friendship Village*, together with other stories sharply critical of parochial attitudes toward Jews and war, apparently without editorial protest.

In this period of her writing life, Gale seems to have confronted something deeply disturbing in small-town America. The year before she published *Peace in Friendship Village* she had been working on *Birth* (1918), a novel that was relatively harsh in its attitude toward small-town life. She also found herself under suspicion in the local community for her persistent antiwar stance. The view of village life that she was evolving was one that could not be successfully managed with generous applications of potted plants, home-baked goods, and common sense. For all intents and purposes, Calliope Marsh was retired from Gale's fiction.

"The Biography of Blade" (1927) acknowledges the potential for a gnawing futility even in so-called successful lives, when they are measured against a cosmopolitan standard. Blade, the hero, is a good deal like Dwight Deacon in the details of his life: he's a respected figure, editor of the local paper, prosperous, with a wife, four children, and even a dyspeptic mother under his roof. He is not the privileged man in this story, but a sympathetic figure whose initial smugness is abruptly unseated by the unexpected "splendor" of beauty and music. The story demonstrates, too, Gale's sensitive consideration of the emotional lives of men.

Blade's fateful encounter with the young guest of his next-door neighbor, who performs at an evening's entertainment in her host's home, is almost comic in its brevity, yet it is affecting, too.

After his one-sided epiphany, Blade begins to respond to his life with greater intensity and longing. Lying rather unheroically on a blanket in his garden, he finds himself drawing closer to death and life. But unsurprisingly, the day ahead brings his flight to its abrupt conclusion and finally to "nameless and infinite loss."

His wife, who is not clearly delineated in the story, seems to read his anguish accurately, though he gives her no clear word or gesture. But her intuitive comment, "'Nobody loves you as I do!'" which, Blade knows, "should have surprised him," cannot do anything to break his fall—the emotional and aesthetic void is too deep.

It is the inexpressible nature of longing, trapped within unrelieved localism, banal social forms, and stilted language, that gives this story its force. Even the ending, in which Blade tries gamely to hold on to something of his dream, partakes of the ridiculous, as his children do not fail to remind him.

The other two stories reprinted in this volume are from a collection titled *Bridal Pond* (1930), which includes stories published in magazines over a seventeen-year period. It is Gale's most accomplished work. In her review of the book, poet Edna Lou Walton called the stories "small masterpieces of character-portrayal and narrative. No other prose writer today has more economy or more polish."

Although Gale herself was not married until relatively late in life, marriage is at the center of a large number of her stories. At the time, marriage was one of the few significant ways in which a woman could change her status. As Gale observed in many of her stories, it is not a simple condition for men either. Both "The Need" and the title story, "Bridal Pond," which won an O. Henry Prize, examine marriage as a harrowing experience. One examines the early stages of marriage, the other its advanced age.

"The Need" describes a single incident, a first party given by a couple, Victoria and Abel Hope, who, with their daughter, are newcomers to a desolate suburb where they know almost no one. Their predicament is touching, the desire to introduce some element of "gracious living" to their tiny house within the general barrenness. With a decidedly naive view of social connections, Abel, the husband, is eager to give a party. In his view, having furnished their home with enviable things gives them the right to entertain.

The disheveled young wife readily accepts the shame and guilt that her fatuous husband heaps upon her as the evening of the party draws closer, and the guest list remains stuck at one. But like Lulu Bett, Victoria is also resourceful and intuitive. She can reach beyond her guilt, as well as her fear of her husband, who has "a temper of unreason and of violence," to apprehend his innocent pride and childlike planning. Her sympathy, more than her shame or dread, galvanizes her. Limited as her options are, she leaves no avenue untried in the pursuit of guests—anybody to be impressed by their possessions as well as the brick ice cream and fancy cakes that Abel has provided.

Victoria's modest triumph occurs at the end, when she not only extends her social situation a bit, but also gives voice to the desperation that has driven her. At last, if only for an instant, "something of her tragedy was clear to Abel," and her husband, shedding the ill-fitting secondhand evening suit he had purchased for the party, responds with admiration and loyalty. Troubled but not hopeless, the situation seems to mirror Gale's abiding concern for the domestic lives of women, circumstances not reflected in her own comfortable life but often an impetus for her attention and activism.

The inspiration for "Bridal Pond" was an accident that occurred in Gale's hometown. A bridal couple, dressed in their wedding outfits and seemingly headed toward their honeymoon or their new life, drove off a fog-bound highway outside of Portage, into a deep pond. They sat dead, drowned, upright in their car, without any indication of a struggle to escape. Gale went to view the accident before the car and the bodies were removed, and she is reported to have said enigmatically, "It's sad—but it isn't dramatic." In linking the tragedy to the marriage of an old couple, Gale created a mysterious, dramatic story.

It begins as Jens Jevins, a prosperous farmer, announces to a hundred stunned spectators in a courtroom that he has murdered his wife of thirty-seven years. The scene is beautifully described as "a ball of glass, in which black figures hang in arrested motion." The words convey not only an image of the courtroom, but also a picture of the drowned couple suspended in the water after the accident.

There is also a suspension of any rational sequencing of events. Jevins has intended to kill his wife, and after "witnessing" the accident, he believes he has. Gale's narrative does not sort out Jevins's confusion between hallucination and reality, using it instead as a metaphor for a state of death in life that is the result of an encroaching disenchantment with marriage, what Jevins calls "the slow rust of unending days." It is a state of affairs to which his wife, Agna, is largely oblivious, save for the fact that she accepts with alacrity his invitation to a late-night walk, since he rarely includes her in such activities anymore. Of course, she does not know, as the reader does, that he intends to drown her.

The townspeople must have their neat solution to the mystery of Jevins's prescience—"The legend grew that Jens Jevins had

had a vision of that happening of the night, and that it had sent him off his head"—but it is limp and explains nothing. Rather, Jevins's words to his wife sound the true paradoxical note: "'I have no need to send you to your death, for we have died in the safety of our youth and not in the deep of days already dead. . . .'"

In the course of the story, the automobile accident is recounted no less than three times. It is as if Gale, like the characters in her story, is struggling to grasp the significance of a tableau, to penetrate its bizarre fusion of the violent and the peaceful, of a beginning that is also an ending. One cannot help wondering whether, in linking the bridal accident with an old couple, Gale was influenced by the fact that it was her father who reported it to her. Was she inspired to wonder what an old man, a fairly recent widower, would think of the event and its connection to the early hopes and promises of marriage? Whatever the confusions Zona Gale experienced in personally responding to the events, she transformed them with a sure hand into a kind of artistic exploration rarely matched elsewhere in her writing.

Zona Gale: A Brief Biography

"I never turned to writing," Zona Gale once said in an interview. "I always squarely faced it."

Gale was born in Portage, Wisconsin, on August 26, 1874, the only child of Eliza and Charles Gale. Both parents would encourage her literary aspirations. Before her marriage, Gale's mother was a teacher and dressmaker; her father was a railroad engineer. Eliza Gale read books to her daughter, participated in her imaginary games, and for the rest of her life was often her daughter's first—though generally uncritical—reader.

But Gale's passion for writing was very much her own. "I wrote when I should have been studying; I wrote through recess, and took home my tablets and wrote." In 1891, when she was seventeen, "Both" was the first of her stories to be published, by *The Evening Wisconsin*.

After graduating from the University of Wisconsin in 1895, Gale moved to Milwaukee, where she became a reporter, first at *The Evening Wisconsin*, then at the *Milwaukee Journal*. Like most women of the period, she covered flower shows, women's club meetings, and the weddings of socially prominent brides; occasionally she also interviewed theatrical figures and reviewed plays.

Discontented with her prospects at the *Journal* and the rejections for the fiction she continued to send out, in 1901 she moved to New York, where she became a reporter at *The New York Evening World*. There she found a market for her stories and published her first novel, *Romance Island* (1906), and several collections of increasingly popular short stories. By the time she won first prize in a *Delineator* magazine short-story contest, which drew fifteen thousand entries, it had become evident that she was earning a comfortable income from her writing, and in 1912 she returned to Portage.

Though the return to Portage was influenced by her mother's repeated pleas, and she would return to New York for a portion of every year, in a significant way it was not a retreat: it coincided with a growing interest in social activism. She became a feminist, a pacifist, a liberal, a supporter of the progressive Wisconsin senator Robert LaFollette, and she pursued civic improvement with the same passion she devoted to her writing.

Gale contributed generously to numerous charities. She became a force for better schools and libraries and became a member of the Board of Regents at the University of Wisconsin. She often wrote and spoke on the need to replace corrupt and ineffective government officials with reformers who would work on behalf of poor and working-class citizens.

A dedicated advocate of women's rights, Gale helped to draft and successfully campaigned for passage of the Wisconsin Equal Rights Law. She was a prominent supporter of the Wisconsin Woman Suffrage Association and the National American Woman Suffrage Association. A founding member of the Women's Peace Party, she served as the national chairwoman of the Civic Department of the General Federation of Women's Clubs, as well as an executive board member of the American Civic Association. She was an early conservationist, a member of the American Civil Liberties Union and the Society for the Advancement of Colored People, an opponent of capital punishment, a supporter of the Children's Aid Society and the Salvation Army, and an advocate for the humane treatment of animals. She also objected to foods using preserved sugar or baked with processed white flour and to the unsanitary conditions common in public places in which food was prepared and sold.

As earnest as she was about her many causes, her sense of humor did not desert her. When a student at one of her lectures asked if she was ever ashamed of anything she wrote, she replied, "Not as often as I should be." In *The Atlantic Monthly* she wrote wryly of the state of coeducation: "Women have minds, too."

Encouraging young writers such as Zora Neale Hurston, Glenway Wescott, and William Maxwell was also one of her missions. She established the Zona Gale Scholarship for talented University of Wisconsin students. Maxwell's reminiscence of her, published in *The Yale Review*, warmly captured her personality and generosity. "I have a theory that behind every artist there is another artist," the *New Yorker* editor and novelist wrote, "that there is a perpetual passing on of talent."

By 1920, Gale had published two novels that most reviewers welcomed as a major and positive change in her subject matter and prose style from sentimentalism to a spare, effective realism. *Birth* (1918) was a critical success; *Miss Lulu Bett* (1920) was an overwhelming commercial success as well. *Miss Lulu Bett* made a strong impression on Brock Pemberton, a Broadway producer, who persuaded Gale to dramatize the novel. She had considered it herself, and now wrote the adaptation and sent it to him in ten days. Pemberton went into production at once, and the play opened to a long run at the Belmont Theater on December 27, 1920.

As originally produced, the play concluded differently from the novel, as Lulu leaves the Deacon household to make her own way in the world as best she can. It was a feminist ending, but not the happy one that audiences were looking for. After a few performances, Gale again adapted the ending and straightened out Ninian's marital status so that his wedding of Lulu turned out to be legitimate. Gale appeared untroubled by the critical clamor about the revisions made in the play, and she wrote a statement saying that she had reverted to the original marriage because her heroine could not marry twice in the course of an evening. It put an end to the controversy, which did not get in the way of her winning the Pulitzer Prize for drama, the first ever awarded to a woman. In 1921 *Miss Lulu Bett* was also made into a film.

❧

In 1928, now a famous and wealthy woman, Zona Gale married for the first time.

In her early years in New York she had fallen in love with Ridgely Torrence, a poet. But as Gale feared, once her parents learned of her suitor, her mother objected to him, suggesting that Torrence was a dreamer without ambition who would allow Zona to support him. (It was an objection that in time became ironic, as Gale's eventual success would purchase a comfortable way of life for her parents.) Gale may have been ambivalent about marriage and motherhood for herself. Cosima, the feminist heroine of her 1917 novel *A Daughter of the Morning*, is frankly uninterested in motherhood:

> And you must see—I'm not a mother-woman. I should love children—to have them, to give them every free chance to grow. But it would be the same with them: their sewing, their mending, a good deal of the care of them—I don't know about it, and I shouldn't like it. I shouldn't be wise about their feeding, or the care of them if they were sick. And as for saying that the knowledge comes with the physical birth of the child, that's sheer nonsense.

Some years after the dissolution of her relationship with Torrence, Gale chose to live with her parents in a household where she was freed from domestic responsibilities and encouraged to continue her writing career without interruption.

William Breese, the man she married in October 1928, was a Portage banker and businessman whom she had known since childhood. The couple each brought an adopted child to the marriage, Juliette, from Breese's first marriage, and Leslyn, a toddler whom Gale had adopted.

After her mother died in 1923, Zona Gale's novels became more mystical. Gale transcribed hundreds of messages that she believed had been sent to her from beyond the grave. These promised that Eliza was close by, protecting and loving. Gale's aesthetic shift appeared to be a longing for transcendence, a wish to no longer have to confront the imperfections of the world. In any event, it lost Gale some of her following among critics and readers.

To the end of her life, however, she was an eminent person. The last known photograph of her is at the 1938 Green Bay Peace Conference sponsored by the Women's International League for Peace and Freedom. It seems fitting that in this group picture, she is standing next to Eleanor Roosevelt.

She died in December of 1938, of pneumonia.

MISS LULU BETT

CONTENTS

I

April

The Deacons were at supper. In the middle of the table was a small, appealing tulip plant, looking as anything would look whose sun was a gas jet. This gas jet was high above the table and flared, with a sound.

"Better turn down the gas jest a little," Mr. Deacon said, and stretched up to do so. He made this joke almost every night. He seldom spoke as a man speaks who has something to say, but as a man who makes something to say.

"Well, what have we on the festive board to-night?" he questioned, eyeing it. "Festive" was his favourite adjective. "Beautiful," too. In October he might be heard asking: "Where's my beautiful fall coat?"

"We have creamed salmon," replied Mrs. Deacon gently. "On toast," she added, with a scrupulous regard for the whole truth. Why she should say this so gently no one can tell. She says everything gently. Her "Could you leave me another bottle of milk this morning?" would wring a milkman's heart.

"Well, now, let us see," said Mr. Deacon, and attacked the principal dish benignly. "*Let* us see," he added, as he served.

"I don't want any," said Monona.

The child Monona was seated upon a book and a cushion, so that her little triangle of nose rose adultly above her plate. Her remark produced precisely the effect for which she had passionately hoped.

"*What's* this?" cried Mr. Deacon. "*No* salmon?"

"No," said Monona, inflected up, chin pertly pointed. She felt her power, discarded her "sir."

"Oh now, Pet!" from Mrs. Deacon, on three notes. "You liked it before."

"I don't want any," said Monona, in precisely her original tone.

"Just a little? A very little?" Mr. Deacon persuaded, spoon dripping.

The child Monona made her lips thin and straight and shook her head until her straight hair flapped in her eyes on either side. Mr. Deacon's eyes anxiously consulted his wife's eyes. What is this? Their progeny will not eat? What can be supplied?

"Some bread and milk!" cried Mrs. Deacon brightly, exploding on "bread." One wondered how she thought of it.

"No," said Monona, inflection up, chin the same. She was affecting indifference to this scene, in which her soul delighted. She twisted her head, bit her lips unconcernedly, and turned her eyes to the remote.

There emerged from the fringe of things, where she perpetually hovered, Mrs. Deacon's older sister, Lulu Bett, who was "making her home with us." And that was precisely the case. *They* were not making her a home, goodness knows. Lulu was the family beast of burden.

"Can't I make her a little milk toast?" she asked Mrs. Deacon.

Mrs. Deacon hesitated, not with compunction at accepting Lulu's offer, not diplomatically to lure Monona. But she hesitated habitually, by nature, as another is by nature vivacious or brunette.

"Yes!" shouted the child Monona.

The tension relaxed. Mrs. Deacon assented. Lulu went to the kitchen. Mr. Deacon served on. Something of this scene was enacted every day. For Monona the drama never lost its zest. It never occurred to the others to let her sit without eating, once, as a cure-all. The Deacons were devoted parents and the child Monona was delicate. She had a white, grave face, white hair, white eyebrows, white lashes. She was sullen, anæmic. They let her wear rings. She "toed in." The poor child was the late birth of a late marriage and the principal joy which she had provided them thus far was the pleased reflection that they had produced her at all.

"Where's your mother, Ina?" Mr. Deacon inquired. "Isn't she coming to her supper?"

"Tantrim," said Mrs. Deacon, softly.

"Oh, ho," said he, and said no more.

The temper of Mrs. Bett, who also lived with them, had days of high vibration when she absented herself from the table as a kind of self-indulgence, and no one could persuade her to food. "Tantrims," they called these occasions.

"Baked potatoes," said Mr. Deacon. "That's good—that's good. The baked potato contains more nourishment than potatoes prepared in any other way. The nourishment is next to the skin. Roasting retains it."

"That's what I always think," said his wife pleasantly.

For fifteen years they had agreed about this.

They ate, in the indecent silence of first savouring food. A delicate crunching of crust, an odour of baked-potato shells, the slip and touch of the silver.

"Num, num, nummy-num!" sang the child Monona loudly, and was hushed by both parents in simultaneous exclamation which rivalled this lyric outburst. They were alone at table. Di, daughter of a wife early lost to Mr. Deacon, was not there. Di was hardly ever there. She was at that age. That age, in Warbleton.

A clock struck the half hour.

"It's curious," Mr. Deacon observed, "how that clock loses. It must be fully quarter to." He consulted his watch. "It is quarter to!" he exclaimed with satisfaction. "I'm pretty good at guessing time."

"I've noticed that!" cried his Ina.

"Last night, it was only twenty-three to, when the half hour struck," he reminded her.

"Twenty-one, I thought." She was tentative, regarded him with arched eyebrows, mastication suspended.

This point was never to be settled. The colloquy was interrupted by the child Monona, whining for her toast. And the doorbell rang.

"Dear me!" said Mr. Deacon. "What can anybody be thinking of to call just at meal-time?"

He trod the hall, flung open the street door. Mrs. Deacon listened. Lulu, coming in with the toast, was warned to silence by an uplifted finger. She deposited the toast, tiptoed to her chair. A withered baked potato and cold creamed salmon were on her plate. The child Monona ate with shocking appreciation. Nothing could be made of the voices in the hall. But Mrs. Bett's door was heard softly to unlatch. She, too, was listening.

A ripple of excitement was caused in the dining-room when Mr. Deacon was divined to usher some one to the parlour. Mr. Deacon would speak with this visitor in a few moments, and now returned to his table. It was notable how slight a thing would give him a sense of self-importance. Now he felt himself a man of affairs, could not even have a quiet supper with his family without the outside world demanding him. He waved his hand to indicate it was nothing which they would know anything about, resumed his seat, served himself to a second spoon of salmon and remarked, "More roast duck, anybody?" in a loud voice and with a slow wink at his wife. That lady at first looked blank, as she always did in the presence of any humour couched with the least indirection, and then drew back her chin and caught her lower lip in her gold-filled teeth. This was her conjugal rebuking.

Swedenborg always uses "conjugial." And really this sounds more married. It should be used with reference to the Deacons. No one was ever more married than they—at least than Mr. Deacon. He made little conjugal jokes in the presence of Lulu who, now completely unnerved by the habit, suspected them where they did not exist, feared lurking *entendre* in the most innocent comments, and became more tense every hour of her life.

And now the eye of the master of the house fell for the first time upon the yellow tulip in the centre of his table.

"Well, *well*!" he said. "What's this?"

Ina Deacon produced, fleetly, an unlooked-for dimple.

"Have you been buying flowers?" the master inquired.

"Ask Lulu," said Mrs. Deacon.

He turned his attention full upon Lulu.

"Suitors?" he inquired, and his lips left their places to form a sort of ruff about the word.

Lulu flushed, and her eyes and their very brows appealed.

"It was a quarter," she said. "There'll be five flowers."

"You *bought* it?"

"Yes. There'll be five—that's a nickel apiece."

His tone was as methodical as if he had been talking about the bread.

"Yet we give you a home on the supposition that you have no money to spend, even for the necessities."

His voice, without resonance, cleft air, thought, spirit, and even flesh.

Mrs. Deacon, indeterminately feeling her guilt in having let loose the dogs of her husband upon Lulu, interposed: "Well, but, Herbert—Lulu isn't strong enough to work. What's the use. . . ."

She dwindled. For years the fiction had been sustained that Lulu, the family beast of burden, was not strong enough to work anywhere else.

"The justice business—" said Dwight Herbert Deacon—he was a justice of the peace—"and the dental profession—" he was also a dentist—"do not warrant the purchase of spring flowers in my home."

"Well, but, Herbert—" It was his wife again.

"No more," he cried briefly, with a slight bend of his head. "Lulu meant no harm," he added, and smiled at Lulu.

There was a moment's silence into which Monona injected a loud "Num, num, nummy-num," as if she were the burden of an Elizabethan lyric. She seemed to close the incident. But the burden was cut off untimely. There was, her father reminded her portentously, company in the parlour.

"When the bell rang, I was so afraid something had happened to Di," said Ina sighing.

"Let's see," said Di's father. "Where is little daughter tonight?"

He must have known that she was at Jenny Plow's at a tea party, for at noon they had talked of nothing else; but this was his way. And Ina played his game, always. She informed him, dutifully.

"Oh, *ho*," said he, absently. How could he be expected to keep his mind on these domestic trifles.

"We told you that this noon," said Lulu. He frowned, disregarded her. Lulu had no delicacy.

"How much is salmon the can now?" he inquired abruptly—this was one of his forms of speech, the can, the pound, the cord.

His partner supplied this information with admirable promptness. Large size, small size, present price, former price—she had them all.

"Dear me," said Mr. Deacon. "That is very nearly salmoney, isn't it?"

"Herbert!" his Ina admonished, in gentle, gentle reproach. Mr. Deacon punned, organically. In talk he often fell silent and then asked some question, schemed to permit his vice to flourish. Mrs. Deacon's return was always automatic: "*Her*bert!"

"Whose Bert?" he said to this. "I thought I was your Bert."

She shook her little head. "You are a case," she told him. He beamed upon her. It was his intention to be a case.

Lulu ventured in upon this pleasantry, and cleared her throat. She was not hoarse, but she was always clearing her throat.

"The butter is about all gone," she observed. "Shall I wait for the butter-woman or get some creamery?"

Mr. Deacon now felt his little jocularities lost before a wall of the matter of fact. He was not pleased. He saw himself as the light of his home, bringer of brightness, lightener of dull hours. It was a pretty rôle. He insisted upon it. To maintain it intact, it was necessary to turn upon their sister with concentrated irritation.

"Kindly settle these matters without bringing them to my attention at mealtime," he said icily.

Lulu flushed and was silent. She was an olive woman, once handsome, now with flat, bluish shadows under her wistful eyes. And if only she would look at her brother Herbert and say something. But she looked in her plate.

"I want some honey," shouted the child, Monona.

"There isn't any, pet," said Lulu.

"I want some," said Monona, eyeing her stonily. But she found that her hair-ribbon could be pulled forward to meet her lips, and she embarked on the biting of an end. Lulu departed for some sauce and cake. It was apple sauce. Mr. Deacon remarked that the apples were almost as good as if he had stolen them. He was giving the impression that he was an irrepressible fellow. He was eating very slowly. It added pleasantly to his sense of importance to feel that some one, there in the parlour, was waiting his motion.

At length they rose. Monona flung herself upon her father. He put her aside firmly, every inch the father. No, no. Father was occupied now. Mrs. Deacon coaxed her away. Monona encircled her mother's waist, lifted her own feet from the floor and hung upon her. "She's such an active child," Lulu ventured brightly.

"Not unduly active, I think," her brother-in-law observed.

He turned upon Lulu his bright smile, lifted his eyebrows, dropped his lids, stood for a moment contemplating the yellow tulip, and so left the room.

Lulu cleared the table. Mrs. Deacon essayed to wind the clock. Well now. Did Herbert say it was twenty-three to-night when it struck the half hour and twenty-one last night, or twenty-one to-night and last night twenty-three? She talked of it as they cleared the table, but Lulu did not talk.

"Can't you remember?" Mrs. Deacon said at last. "I should think you might be useful."

Lulu was lifting the yellow tulip to set it on the sill. She changed her mind. She took the plant to the wood-shed and tumbled it with force upon the chip-pile.

The dining-room table was laid for breakfast. The two women brought their work and sat there. The child Monona hung miserably about, watching the clock. Right or wrong, she was put to bed by it. She had eight minutes more—seven—six—five—

Lulu laid down her sewing and left the room. She went to the wood-shed, groped about in the dark, found the stalk of the one tulip flower in its heap on the chip-pile. The tulip she fastened in her gown on her flat chest.

Outside were to be seen the early stars. It is said that if our sun were as near to Arcturus as we are near to our sun, the great Arcturus would burn our sun to nothingness.

In the Deacons' parlour sat Bobby Larkin, eighteen. He was in pain all over. He was come on an errand which civilisation has contrived to make an ordeal.

Before him on the table stood a photograph of Diana Deacon, also eighteen. He hated her with passion. At school she mocked him, aped him, whispered about him, tortured him. For two years he had hated her. Nights he fell asleep planning to build a great house and engage her as its servant.

Yet, as he waited, he could not keep his eyes from this photograph. It was Di at her curliest, at her fluffiest, Di conscious of her bracelet, Di smiling. Bobby gazed, his basic aversion to her hard-pressed by a most reluctant pleasure. He hoped that he would not see her, and he listened for her voice.

Mr. Deacon descended upon him with an air carried from his supper hour, bland, dispensing. Well! Let us have it. "What did you wish to see me about?"—with a use of the past tense as connoting something of indirection and hence of delicacy—a nicety customary, yet unconscious. Bobby had arrived in his best clothes and with an air of such formality that Mr. Deacon had instinctively suspected him of wanting to join the church, and, to treat the time with due solemnity, had put him in the parlour until he could attend at leisure.

Confronted thus by Di's father, the speech which Bobby had planned deserted him.

"I thought if you would give me a job," he said defencelessly.

"So that's it!" Mr. Deacon, who always awaited but a touch to be either irritable or facetious, inclined now to be facetious. "Filling teeth?" he would know. "Marrying folks, then?" Assistant justice or assistant dentist—which?

Bobby blushed. No, no, but in that big building of Mr. Deacon's where his office was, wasn't there something . . . It faded from him, sounded ridiculous. Of course there was nothing. He saw it now.

There was nothing. Mr. Deacon confirmed him. But Mr. Deacon had an idea. Hold on, he said—hold on. The grass. Would Bobby consider taking charge of the grass? Though Mr. Deacon was of the type which cuts its own grass and glories in its vigour and its energy, yet in the time after that which he called "dental hours" Mr. Deacon wished to work in his garden. His grass, growing in late April rains, would need attention early next month . . . he owned two lots—"of course property *is* a burden." If Bobby would care to keep the grass down and raked . . . Bobby would care, accepted this business opportunity, figures and all, thanked Mr. Deacon with earnestness. Bobby's aversion to Di, it seemed, should not stand in the way of his advancement.

"Then that is checked off," said Mr. Deacon heartily.

Bobby wavered toward the door, emerged on the porch, and ran almost upon Di returning from her tea party at Jenny Plow's.

"Oh, Bobby! You came to see me?"

She was as fluffy, as curly, as smiling as her picture. She was carrying pink, gauzy favours and a spear of flowers. Undeniably in her voice there was pleasure. Her glance was startled but already complacent. She paused on the steps, a lovely figure.

But one would say that nothing but the truth dwelt in Bobby.

"Oh, hullo," said he. "No. I came to see your father."

He marched by her. His hair stuck up at the back. His coat was hunched about his shoulders. His insufficient nose, abundant, loose-lipped mouth and brown eyes were completely expressionless. He marched by her without a glance.

She flushed with vexation. Mr. Deacon, as one would expect, laughed loudly, took the situation in his elephantine grasp and pawed at it.

"Mamma! Mamma! What do you s'pose? Di thought she had a beau—"

"Oh, papa!" said Di. "Why, I just hate Bobby Larkin and the whole *school* knows it."

Mr. Deacon returned to the dining-room, humming in his throat. He entered upon a pretty scene.

His Ina was darning. Four minutes of grace remaining to the child Monona, she was spinning on one toe with some Bacchanalian idea of making the most of the present. Di dominated, her ruffles, her blue hose, her bracelet, her ring.

"Oh, and mamma," she said, "the sweetest party and the dearest supper and the darlingest decorations and the gorgeousest—"

"Grammar, grammar," spoke Dwight Herbert Deacon. He

was not sure what he meant, but the good fellow felt some violence done somewhere or other.

"Well," said Di positively, "they *were*. Papa, see my favour."

She showed him a sugar dove, and he clucked at it.

Ina glanced at them fondly, her face assuming its loveliest light. She was often ridiculous, but always she was the happy wife and mother, and her rôle reduced her individual absurdities at least to its own.

The door to the bedroom now opened and Mrs. Bett appeared.

"Well, mother!" cried Herbert, the "well" curving like an arm, the "mother" descending like a brisk slap. "Hungry *now*?"

Mrs. Bett was hungry now. She had emerged intending to pass through the room without speaking and find food in the pantry. By obscure processes her son-in-law's tone inhibited all this.

"No," she said. "I'm not hungry."

Now that she was there, she seemed uncertain what to do. She looked from one to another a bit hopelessly, somehow foiled in her dignity. She brushed at her skirt, the veins of her long, wrinkled hands catching an intenser blue from the dark cloth. She put her hair behind her ears.

"We put a potato in the oven for you," said Ina. She had never learned quite how to treat these periodic refusals of her mother to eat, but she never had ceased to resent them.

"No, thank you," said Mrs. Bett. Evidently she rather enjoyed the situation, creating for herself a spot-light much in the manner of Monona.

"Mother," said Lulu, "let me make you some toast and tea."

Mrs. Bett turned her gentle, bloodless face toward her daughter, and her eyes warmed.

"After a little, maybe," she said. "I think I'll run over to see Grandma Gates now," she added, and went toward the door.

"Tell her," cried Dwight, "tell her she's my best girl."

Grandma Gates was a rheumatic cripple who lived next door, and whenever the Deacons or Mrs. Bett were angry or hurt or wished to escape the house for some reason, they stalked over to Grandma Gates—in lieu of, say, slamming a door. These visits radiated an almost daily friendliness which lifted and tempered the old invalid's lot and life.

Di flashed out at the door again, on some trivial permission.

"A good many of mamma's stitches in that dress to keep clean," Ina called after.

"Early, darling, early!" her father reminded her. A faint regurgitation of his was somehow invested with the paternal.

"What's this?" cried Dwight Herbert Deacon abruptly.

On the clock shelf lay a letter.

"Oh, Dwight!" Ina was all compunction. "It came this morning. I forgot."

"I forgot it too! And I laid it up there." Lulu was eager for her share of the blame.

"Isn't it understood that my mail can't wait like this?"

Dwight's sense of importance was now being fed in gulps.

"I know. I'm awfully sorry," Lulu said, "but you hardly ever get a letter—"

This might have made things worse, but it provided Dwight with a greater importance.

"Of course, pressing matter goes to my office," he admitted it. "Still, my mail should have more careful—"

He read, frowning. He replaced the letter, and they hung upon his motions as he tapped the envelope and regarded them.

"Now!" said he. "What do you think I have to tell you?"

"Something nice," Ina was sure.

"Something surprising," Dwight said portentously.

"But, Dwight—is it *nice*?" from his Ina.

"That depends. I like it. So'll Lulu." He leered at her. "It's company."

"Oh, Dwight," said Ina. "Who?"

"From Oregon," he said, toying with his suspense.

"Your brother!" cried Ina. "Is he coming?"

"Yes. Ninian's coming, so he says."

"Ninian!" cried Ina again. She was excited, round-eyed, her moist lips parted. Dwight's brother Ninian. How long was it? Nineteen years. South America, Central America, Mexico, Panama "and all." When was he coming and what was he coming for?

"To see me," said Dwight. "To meet you. Some day next week. He don't know what a charmer Lulu is, or he'd come quicker."

Lulu flushed terribly. Not from the implication. But from the knowledge that she was not a charmer.

The clock struck. The child Monona uttered a cutting shriek. Herbert's eyes flew not only to the child but to his wife. What was this, was their progeny hurt?

"Bedtime," his wife elucidated, and added: "Lulu, will you take her to bed? I'm pretty tired."

Lulu rose and took Monona by the hand, the child hanging back and shaking her straight hair in an unconvincing negative.

As they crossed the room, Dwight Herbert Deacon, strolling about and snapping his fingers, halted and cried out sharply:

"Lulu. One moment!"

He approached her. A finger was extended, his lips were parted, on his forehead was a frown.

"You *picked* the flower on the plant?" he asked incredulously.

Lulu made no reply. But the child Monona felt herself lifted and borne to the stairway and the door was shut with violence. On the dark stairway Lulu's arms closed about her in an embrace which left her breathless and squeaking. And yet Lulu was not really fond of the child Monona, either. This was a discharge of emotion akin, say, to slamming the door.

II

May

Lulu was dusting the parlour. The parlour was rarely used, but every morning it was dusted. By Lulu.

She dusted the black walnut centre table which was of Ina's choosing, and looked like Ina, shining, complacent, abundantly curved. The leather rocker, too, looked like Ina, brown, plumply upholstered, tipping back a bit. Really, the davenport looked like Ina, for its chintz pattern seemed to bear a design of lifted eyebrows and arch, reproachful eyes.

Lulu dusted the upright piano, and that was like Dwight—in a perpetual attitude of rearing back, with paws out, playful, but capable, too, of roaring a ready bass.

And the black fireplace—there was Mrs. Bett to the life. Colourless, fireless, and with a dust of ashes.

In the midst of all was Lulu herself reflected in the narrow pier glass, bodiless-looking in her blue gingham gown, but somehow alive. Natural.

This pier glass Lulu approached with expectation, not because of herself but because of the photograph on its low marble shelf.

A large photograph on a little shelf-easel. A photograph of a man with evident eyes, evident lips, evident cheeks—and each of the six were rounded and convex. You could construct the rest of him. Down there under the glass you could imagine him extending, rounded and convex, with plump hands and curly thumbs and snug clothes. It was Ninian Deacon, Dwight's brother.

Every day since his coming had been announced Lulu, dusting the parlour, had seen the photograph looking at her with its eyes somehow new. Or were her own eyes new? She dusted this photograph with a difference, lifted, dusted, set it back, less as a process than as an experience. As she dusted the mirror and saw his trim semblance over against her own bodiless reflection, she hurried away. But the eyes of the picture followed her, and she liked it.

She dusted the south window-sill and saw Bobby Larkin come round the house and go to the wood-shed for the lawn mower. She heard the smooth blur of the cutter. Not six times had Bobby traversed the lawn when Lulu saw Di emerge from the house. Di had been caring for her canary and she carried her bird-bath and went to the well, and Lulu divined that Di had deliberately disregarded the handy kitchen taps. Lulu dusted the south window and watched, and in her watching was no quality of spying or of criticism. Nor did she watch wistfully. Rather, she looked out on something in which she had never shared, could not by any chance imagine herself sharing.

The south windows were open. Airs of May bore the soft talking.

"Oh, Bobby, will you pump while I hold this?" And again: "Now wait till I rinse." And again: "You needn't be so glum"—the village salutation signifying kindly attention.

Bobby now first spoke: "Who's glum?" he countered gloomily.

The iron of those days when she had laughed at him was deep within him, and this she now divined, and said absently:

"I used to think you were pretty nice. But I don't like you any more."

"Yes, you used to!" Bobby repeated derisively. "Is that why you made fun of me all the time?"

At this Di coloured and tapped her foot on the well-curb. He seemed to have her now, and enjoyed his triumph. But Di looked up at him shyly and looked down. "I had to," she admitted. "They were all teasing me about you."

"They were?" This was a new thought to him. Teasing her about him, were they? He straightened. "Huh!" he said, in magnificent evasion.

"I had to make them stop, so I teased you. I—I never wanted to." Again the upward look.

"Well!" Bobby stared at her. "I never thought it was anything like that."

"Of course you didn't." She tossed back her bright hair, met his eyes full. "And you never came where I could tell you. I wanted to tell you."

She ran into the house.

Lulu lowered her eyes. It was as if she had witnessed the exercise of some secret gift, had seen a cocoon open or an egg hatch. She was thinking:

"How easy she done it. Got him right over. But *how* did she do that?"

Dusting the Dwight-like piano, Lulu looked over-shoulder, with a manner of speculation, at the photograph of Ninian.

Bobby mowed and pondered. The magnificent conceit of the male in his understanding of the female character was sufficiently developed to cause him to welcome the improvisation which he had just heard. Perhaps that was the way it had been. Of course that was the way it had been. What a fool he had been not to understand. He cast his eyes repeatedly toward the house. He managed to make the job last over so that he could return in the afternoon. He was not conscious of planning this, but it was in some manner contrived for him by forces of his own with which he seemed to be coöperating without his conscious will. Continually he glanced toward the house.

These glances Lulu saw. She was a woman of thirty-four and Di and Bobby were eighteen, but Lulu felt for them no adult indulgence. She felt that sweetness of attention which we bestow upon May robins. She felt more.

She cut a fresh cake, filled a plate, called to Di, saying: "Take some out to that Bobby Larkin, why don't you?"

It was Lulu's way of participating. It was her vicarious thrill.

After supper Dwight and Ina took their books and departed to the Chautauqua Circle. To these meetings Lulu never went. The reason seemed to be that she never went anywhere.

When they were gone Lulu felt an instant liberation. She turned aimlessly to the garden and dug round things with her finger. And she thought about the brightness of that Chautauqua scene to which Ina and Dwight had gone. Lulu thought about such gatherings in somewhat the way that a futurist receives the subjects of his art—forms not vague, but heightened to intolerable definiteness, acute colour, and always motion—motion as an integral part of the desirable. But a factor of all was that Lulu herself was the participant, not the onlooker. The perfection of her dream was not impaired by any longing. She had her dream as a saint her sense of heaven.

"Lulie!" her mother called. "You come out of that damp."

She obeyed, as she had obeyed that voice all her life. But she took one last look down the dim street. She had not known it, but superimposed on her Chautauqua thoughts had been her faint hope that it would be to-night, while she was in the garden alone, that Ninian Deacon would arrive. And she had on her wool chally, her coral beads, her cameo pin. . . .

She went into the lighted dining-room. Monona was in bed. Di was not there. Mrs. Bett was in Dwight Herbert's leather chair and she lolled at her ease. It was strange to see this woman, usually so erect and tense, now actually lolling, as if lolling were the positive, the vital, and her ordinary rigidity a negation of her. In some corresponding orgy of leisure and liberation, Lulu sat down with no needle.

"Inie ought to make over her delaine," Mrs. Bett comfortably began. They talked of this, devised a mode, recalled other delaines. "Dear, dear," said Mrs. Bett, "I had on a delaine when I met your father." She described it. Both women talked freely, with animation. They were individuals and alive. To the two pallid beings accessory to the Deacons' presence, Mrs. Bett and her daughter Lulu now bore no relationship. They emerged, had opinions, contradicted, their eyes were bright.

Toward nine o'clock Mrs. Bett announced that she thought she should have a lunch. This was debauchery. She brought in bread-and-butter, and a dish of cold canned peas. She was committing all the excesses that she knew—offering opinions, laughing, eating. It was to be seen that this woman had an immense store of vitality, perpetually submerged.

When she had eaten she grew sleepy—rather cross at the last and inclined to hold up her sister's excellencies to Lulu; and, at Lulu's defence, lifted an ancient weapon.

"What's the use of finding fault with Inie? Where'd you been if she hadn't married?"

Lulu said nothing.

"What say?" Mrs. Bett demanded shrilly. She was enjoying it.

Lulu said no more. After a long time:

"You always was jealous of Inie," said Mrs. Bett, and went to her bed.

As soon as her mother's door had closed, Lulu took the lamp from its bracket, stretching up her long body and her long arms until her skirt lifted to show her really slim and pretty feet. Lulu's feet gave news of some other Lulu, but slightly incarnate. Perhaps, so far, incarnate only in her feet and her long hair.

She took the lamp to the parlour and stood before the photograph of Ninian Deacon, and looked her fill. She did not admire the photograph, but she wanted to look at it. The house was still, there was no possibility of interruption. The occasion became sensation, which she made no effort to quench. She held a rendezvous with she knew not what.

In the early hours of the next afternoon with the sun shining across the threshold, Lulu was paring something at the kitchen table. Mrs. Bett was asleep. ("I don't blame you a bit, mother," Lulu had said, as her mother named the intention.) Ina was asleep. (But Ina always took off the curse by calling it her "siesta," long *i*.) Monona was playing with a neighbour's child—you heard their shrill yet lovely laughter as they obeyed the adult law that motion is pleasure. Di was not there.

A man came round the house and stood tying a puppy to the porch post. A long shadow fell through the west doorway, the puppy whined.

"Oh," said this man. "I didn't mean to arrive at the back door, but since I'm here—"

He lifted a suitcase to the porch, entered, and filled the kitchen.

"It's Ina, isn't it?" he said.

"I'm her sister," said Lulu, and understood that he was here at last.

"Well, I'm Bert's brother," said Ninian. "So I can come in, can't I?"

He did so, turned round like a dog before his chair and sat down heavily, forcing his fingers through heavy, upspringing brown hair.

"Oh, yes," said Lulu. "I'll call Ina. She's asleep."

"Don't call her, then," said Ninian. "Let's you and I get acquainted."

He said it absently, hardly looking at her.

"I'll get the pup a drink if you can spare me a basin," he added.

Lulu brought the basin, and while he went to the dog she ran tiptoeing to the dining-room china closet and brought a cut-glass tumbler, as heavy, as ungainly as a stone crock. This she filled with milk.

"I thought maybe . . ." said she, and offered it.

"Thank *you!*" said Ninian, and drained it. "Making pies, as I live," he observed, and brought his chair nearer to the table. "I didn't know Ina had a sister," he went on. "I remember now Bert said he had two of her relatives—"

Lulu flushed and glanced at him pitifully.

"He has," she said. "It's my mother and me. But we do quite a good deal of the work."

"I'll bet you do," said Ninian, and did not perceive that anything had been violated. "What's your name?" he bethought.

She was in an immense and obscure excitement. Her manner was serene, her hands as they went on with the peeling did not tremble; her replies were given with sufficient quiet. But she told him her name as one tells something of another and more remote creature. She felt as one may feel in catastrophe—no sharp understanding but merely the sense that the thing cannot possibly be happening.

"You folks expect me?" he went on.

"Oh, yes," she cried, almost with vehemence. "Why, we've looked for you every day."

"'See," he said, "how long have they been married?"

Lulu flushed as she answered: "Fifteen years."

"And a year before that the first one died—and two years they were married," he computed. "I never met that one. Then it's close to twenty years since Bert and I have seen each other."

"How awful," Lulu said, and flushed again.

"Why?"

"To be that long away from your folks."

Suddenly she found herself facing this honestly, as if the immensity of her present experience were clarifying her understanding: Would it be so awful to be away from Bert and Monona and Di—yes, and Ina, for twenty years?

"You think that?" he laughed. "A man don't know what he's like till he's roamed around on his own." He liked the sound of it. "Roamed around on his own," he repeated, and laughed again. "Course a woman don't know that."

"Why don't she?" asked Lulu. She balanced a pie on her hand and carved the crust. She was stupefied to hear her own question. "Why don't she?"

"Maybe she does. Do you?"

"Yes," said Lulu.

"Good enough!" He applauded noiselessly, with fat hands. His diamond ring sparkled, his even white teeth flashed. "I've had twenty years of galloping about," he informed her, unable, after all, to transfer his interests from himself to her.

"Where?" she asked, although she knew.

"South America. Central America. Mexico. Panama." He searched his memory. "Colombo," he superadded.

"My!" said Lulu. She had probably never in her life had the least desire to see any of these places. She did not want to see them now. But she wanted passionately to meet her companion's mind.

"It's the life," he informed her.

"Must be," Lulu breathed. "I—" she tried, and gave it up.

"Where you been mostly?" he asked at last.

By this unprecedented interest in her doings she was thrown into a passion of excitement.

"Here," she said. "I've always been here. Fifteen years with Ina. Before that we lived in the country."

He listened sympathetically now, his head well on one side. He watched her veined hands pinch at the pies. "Poor old girl," he was thinking.

"Is it Miss Lulu Bett?" he abruptly inquired. "Or Mrs.?"

Lulu flushed in anguish.

"Miss," she said low, as one who confesses the extremity of failure. Then from unplumbed depths another Lulu abruptly spoke up. "From choice," she said.

He shouted with laughter.

"You bet! Oh, you bet!" he cried. "Never doubted it." He made his palms taut and drummed on the table. "Say!" he said.

Lulu glowed, quickened, smiled. Her face was another face.

"Which kind of a Mr. are you?" she heard herself ask, and his shoutings redoubled. Well! Who would have thought it of her?

"Never give myself away," he assured her. "Say, by George, I never thought of that before! There's no telling whether a man's married or not, by his name!"

"It don't matter," said Lulu.

"Why not?"

"Not so many people want to know."

Again he laughed. This laughter was intoxicating to Lulu. No one ever laughed at what she said save Herbert, who laughed at *her*. "Go it, old girl!" Ninian was thinking, but this did not appear.

The child Monona now arrived, banging the front gate and hurling herself round the house on the board walk, catching the toe of one foot in the heel of the other and blundering forward, head down, her short, straight hair flapping over her face. She landed flat-footed on the porch. She began to speak, using a ridiculous perversion of words, scarcely articulate, then in vogue in her group. And,

"Whose dog?" she shrieked.

Ninian looked over his shoulder, held out his hand, finished something that he was saying to Lulu. Monona came to him readily enough, staring, loose-lipped.

"I'll bet I'm your uncle," said Ninian.

Relationship being her highest known form of romance, Monona was thrilled by this intelligence.

"Give us a kiss," said Ninian, finding in the plural some vague mitigation for some vague offence.

Monona, looking silly, complied. And her uncle said my stars, such a great big tall girl—they would have to put a board on her head.

"What's that?" inquired Monona. She had spied his great diamond ring.

"This," said her uncle, "was brought to me by Santa Claus, who keeps a jewellery shop in heaven."

The precision and speed of his improvisation revealed him. He had twenty other diamonds like this one. He kept them for those Sundays when the sun comes up in the west. Of course—often! Some day he was going to melt a diamond and eat it. Then you sparkled all over in the dark, ever after. Another diamond he was going to plant. They say— He did it all gravely, absorbedly. About it he was as conscienceless as a savage. This was no fancy spun to pleasure a child. This was like lying, for its own sake.

He went on talking with Lulu, and now again he was the tease, the braggart, the unbridled, unmodified male.

Monona stood in the circle of his arm. The little being was attentive, softened, subdued. Some pretty, faint light visited her. In her listening look, she showed herself a charming child.

"It strikes me," said Ninian to Lulu, "that you're going to do something mighty interesting before you die."

It was the clear conversational impulse, born of the need to keep something going, but Lulu was all faith.

She closed the oven door on her pies and stood brushing flour from her fingers. He was looking away from her, and she looked at him. He was completely like his picture. She felt as if she were looking at his picture and she was abashed and turned away.

"Well, I hope so," she said, which had certainly never been true, for her old formless dreams were no intention—nothing but a mush of discontent. "I hope I can do something that's nice before I quit," she said. Nor was this hope now independently true, but only this surprising longing to appear interesting in his eyes. To dance before him. "What would the folks think of me, going on so?" she suddenly said. Her mild sense of disloyalty was delicious. So was his understanding glance.

"You're the stuff," he remarked absently.

She laughed happily.

The door opened. Ina appeared.

"Well!" said Ina. It was her remotest tone. She took this man to be a pedlar, beheld her child in his clasp, made a quick, forward step, chin lifted. She had time for a very javelin of a look at Lulu.

"Hello!" said Ninian. He had the one formula. "I believe I'm your husband's brother. Ain't this Ina?"

It had not crossed the mind of Lulu to present him.

Beautiful it was to see Ina relax, soften, warm, transform, humanise. It gave one hope for the whole species.

"Ninian!" she cried. She lent a faint impression of the double *e* to the initial vowel. She slurred the rest, until the *y* sound squinted in. Not Neenyun, but nearly Neenyun.

He kissed her.

"Since Dwight isn't here!" she cried, and shook her finger at him. Ina's conception of hostess-ship was definite: A volley of questions—was his train on time? He had found the house all right? Of course! Any one could direct him, she should hope. And he hadn't seen Dwight? She must telephone him. But then she arrested herself with a sharp, curved fling of her starched skirts. No! They would surprise him at tea—she stood taut, lips compressed. Oh, the Plows were coming to tea. How unfortunate, she thought. How fortunate, she said.

The child Monona made her knees and elbows stiff and danced up and down. She must, she must participate.

"Aunt Lulu made three pies!" she screamed, and shook her straight hair.

"Gracious sakes," said Ninian. "I brought her a pup, and if I didn't forget to give it to her."

They adjourned to the porch—Ninian, Ina, Monona. The

puppy was presented, and yawned. The party kept on about "the place." Ina delightedly exhibited the tomatoes, the two apple trees, the new shed, the bird-bath. Ninian said the unspellable "m—m," rising inflection, and the "I see," prolonging the verb as was expected of him. Ina said that they meant to build a summer-house, only, dear me, when you have a family—but there, he didn't know anything about that. Ina was using her eyes, she was arch, she was coquettish, she was flirtatious, and she believed herself to be merely matronly, sisterly, womanly. . . .

She screamed. Dwight was at the gate. Now the meeting, exclamation, banality, guffaw . . . good will.

And Lulu, peeping through the blind.

When "tea" had been experienced that evening, it was found that a light rain was falling and the Deacons and their guests, the Plows, were constrained to remain in the parlour. The Plows were gentle, faintly lustrous folk, sketched into life rather lightly, as if they were, say, looking in from some other level.

"The only thing," said Dwight Herbert, "that reconciles me to rain is that I'm let off croquet." He rolled his r's, a favourite device of his to induce humour. He called it "croquette." He had never been more irrepressible. The advent of his brother was partly accountable, the need to show himself a fine family man and host in a prosperous little home—simple and pathetic desire.

"Tell you what we'll do!" said Dwight. "Nin and I'll reminisce a little."

"Do!" cried Mr. Plow. This gentle fellow was always excited by life, so faintly excited by him, and enjoyed its presentation in any real form.

Ninian had unerringly selected a dwarf rocker, and he was overflowing it and rocking.

"Take this chair, do!" Ina begged. "A big chair for a big man." She spoke as if he were about the age of Monona.

Ninian refused, insisted on his refusal. A few years more, and human relationships would have spread sanity even to Ina's estate and she would have told him why he should exchange chairs. As it was she forbore, and kept glancing anxiously at the overburdened little beast beneath him.

The child Monona entered the room. She had been driven down by Di and Jenny Plow, who had vanished upstairs and, through the ventilator, might be heard in a lift and fall of giggling. Monona had also been driven from the kitchen where Lulu was, for some reason, hurrying through the dishes. Monona now ran to Mrs. Bett, stood beside her and stared about resentfully. Mrs. Bett was in best black and ruches, and she seized upon Monona and patted her, as her own form of social expression; and Monona wriggled like a puppy, as hers.

"Quiet, pettie," said Ina, eyebrows up. She caught her lower lip in her teeth.

"Well, sir," said Dwight, "you wouldn't think it to look at us, but mother had her hands pretty full, bringing us up."

Into Dwight's face came another look. It was always so, when he spoke of this foster-mother who had taken these two boys and seen them through the graded schools. This woman Dwight adored, and when he spoke of her he became his inner self.

"We must run up-state and see her while you're here, Nin," he said.

To this Ninian gave a casual assent, lacking his brother's really tender ardour.

"Little," Dwight pursued, "little did she think I'd settle down into a nice, quiet, married dentist and magistrate in my town. And Nin into—say, Nin, what are you, anyway?"

They laughed.

"That's the question," said Ninian.

They laughed.

"Maybe," Ina ventured, "maybe Ninian will tell us something about his travels. He is quite a traveller, you know," she said to the Plows. "A regular Gulliver."

They laughed respectfully.

"How we should love it, Mr. Deacon," Mrs. Plow said. "You know we've never seen *very* much."

Goaded on, Ninian launched upon his foreign countries as he had seen them: Population, exports, imports, soil, irrigation, business. For the populations Ninian had no respect. Crops could not touch ours. Soil mighty poor pickings. And the business—say! Those fellows don't know—and, say, the hotels! Don't say foreign hotel to Ninian.

He regarded all the alien earth as barbarian, and he stoned it. He was equipped for absolutely no intensive observation. His contacts were negligible. Mrs. Plow was more excited by the Deacons' party than Ninian had been wrought upon by all his voyaging.

"Tell you," said Dwight. "When we ran away that time and went to the state fair, little did we think—" He told about running away to the state fair. "I thought," he wound up, irrelevantly, "Ina and I might get over to the other side this year, but I guess not. I guess not."

The words give no conception of their effect, spoken thus. For there in Warbleton these words are not commonplace. In Warbleton, Europe is never so casually spoken. "Take a trip abroad" is the phrase, or "Go to Europe" at the very least, and both with empressement. Dwight had somewhere noted and deliberately picked up that "other side" effect, and his Ina knew this, and was proud. Her covert glance about pensively covered her soft triumph.

Mrs. Bett, her arm still circling the child Monona, now made her first observation.

"Pity not to have went while the going was good," she said, and said no more.

Nobody knew quite what she meant, and everybody hoped for the best. But Ina frowned. Mamma did these things occasionally when there was company, and she dared. She never sauced Dwight in private. And it wasn't fair, it wasn't *fair*—

Abruptly Ninian rose and left the room.

The dishes were washed. Lulu had washed them at break-neck speed—she could not, or would not, have told why. But no sooner were they finished and set away than Lulu had been attacked by an unconquerable inhibition. And instead of going to the parlour, she sat down by the kitchen window. She was in her chally gown, with her cameo pin and her string of coral.

Laughter from the parlour mingled with the laughter of Di and Jenny upstairs. Lulu was now rather shy of Di. A night or two before, coming home with "extra" cream, she had gone round to the side-door and had come full upon Di and Bobby, seated on the steps. And Di was saying:

"Well, if I marry you, you've simply got to be a great man. I could never marry just anybody. I'd *smother*."

Lulu had heard, stricken. She passed them by, responding only faintly to their greeting. Di was far less taken aback than Lulu.

Later Di had said to Lulu: "I s'pose you heard what we were saying."

Lulu, much shaken, had withdrawn from the whole matter by a flat "no." "Because," she said to herself, "I couldn't have heard right."

But since then she had looked at Di as if Di were some one else. Had not Lulu taught her to make buttonholes and to hem—oh, no! Lulu could not have heard properly.

"Everybody's got somebody to be nice to them," she thought now, sitting by the kitchen window, adult yet Cinderella.

She thought that some one would come for her. Her mother or even Ina. Perhaps they would send Monona. She waited at first hopefully, then resentfully. The grey rain wrapped the air.

"Nobody cares what becomes of me after they're fed," she thought, and derived an obscure satisfaction from her phrasing, and thought it again.

Ninian Deacon came into the kitchen.

Her first impression was that he had come to see whether the dog had been fed.

"I fed him," she said, and wished that she had been busy when Ninian entered.

"Who, me?" he asked. "You did that all right. Say, why in time don't you come in the other room?"

"Oh, I don't know."

"Well, neither do I. I've kept thinking, 'Why don't she come along.' Then I remembered the dishes." He glanced about. "I come to help wipe dishes."

"Oh!" she laughed so delicately, so delightfully, one wondered where she got it. "They're washed—" she caught herself at "long ago."

"Well then, what are you doing here?"

"Resting."

"Rest in there." He bowed, crooked his arm. "Señora," he said—his Spanish matched his other assimilations of travel—"Señora. Allow me."

Lulu rose. On his arm she entered the parlour. Dwight was narrating and did not observe that entrance. To the Plows it was sufficiently normal. But Ina looked up and said:

"Well!"—in two notes, descending, curving.

Lulu did not look at her. Lulu sat in a low rocker. Her starched white skirt, throwing her chally in ugly lines, revealed a peeping rim of white embroidery. Her lace front wrinkled when she sat, and perpetually she adjusted it. She curled her feet sidewise beneath her chair, her long wrists and veined hands lay along her lap in no relation to her. She was tense. She rocked.

When Dwight had finished his narration, there was a pause, broken at last by Mrs. Bett:

"You tell that better than you used to when you started in telling it," she observed. "You got in some things I guess you used to clean forget about. Monona, get off my rocker."

Monona made a little whimpering sound, in pretence to tears. Ina said, "Darling—quiet!"—chin a little lifted, lower lip revealing lower teeth for the word's completion; and she held it.

The Plows were asking something about Mexico. Dwight was wondering if it would let up raining *at all*. Di and Jenny came whispering into the room. But all these distractions Ninian Deacon swept aside.

"Miss Lulu," he said, "I wanted you to hear about my trip up the Amazon, because I knew how inter-ested you are in travels."

He talked, according to his lights, about the Amazon. But the person who most enjoyed the recital could not afterward have told two words that he said. Lulu kept the position which she had taken at first, and she dare not change. She saw the blood in the veins of her hands and wanted to hide them. She wondered if she might fold her arms, or have one hand to support her chin, gave it all up and sat motionless, save for the rocking.

Then she forgot everything. For the first time in years some one was talking and looking not only at Ina and Dwight and their guests, but at her.

III

June

On a June morning Dwight Herbert Deacon looked at the sky, and said with his manner of originating it:

"How about a picnic this afternoon?"

Ina, with her blank, upward look, exclaimed: "To-*day*?"

"First class day, it looks like to me."

Come to think of it, Ina didn't know that there was anything to prevent, but mercy, Herbert was so sudden. Lulu began to recite the resources of the house for a lunch. Meanwhile, since the first mention of picnic, the child Monona had been dancing stiffly about the room, knees stiff, elbows stiff, shoulders immovable, her straight hair flapping about her face. The sad dance of the child who cannot dance because she never has danced. Di gave a conservative assent—she was at that age—and then took advantage of the family softness incident to a guest and demanded that Bobby go too. Ina hesitated, partly because she always hesitated, partly because she was tribal in the extreme. "Just our little family and Uncle Ninian would have been so nice," she sighed, with her consent.

When, at six o'clock, Ina and Dwight and Ninian assembled on the porch and Lulu came out with the basket, it was seen that she was in a blue-cotton house-gown.

"Look here," said Ninian, "aren't you going?"

"Me?" said Lulu. "Oh, no."

"Why not?"

"Oh, I haven't been to a picnic since I can remember."

"But why not?"

"Oh, I never think of such a thing."

Ninian waited for the family to speak. They did speak. Dwight said:

"Lulu's a regular home body."

And Ina advanced kindly with: "Come with us, Lulu, if you like."

"No," said Lulu, and flushed. "Thank you," she added, formally.

Mrs. Bett's voice shrilled from within the house, startlingly close—just beyond the blind, in fact:

"Go on, Lulie. It'll do you good. You mind me and go on."

"Well," said Ninian, "that's what I say. You hustle for your hat and you come along."

For the first time this course presented itself to Lulu as a possibility. She stared up at Ninian.

"You can slip on my linen duster, over," Ina said graciously.

"Your new one?" Dwight incredulously wished to know.

"Oh, no!" Ina laughed at the idea. "The old one."

They were having to wait for Di in any case—they always had to wait for Di—and at last, hardly believing in her own motions, Lulu was running to make ready. Mrs. Bett hurried to help her, but she took down the wrong things and they were both irritated. Lulu reappeared in the linen duster and a wide hat. There had been no time to "tighten up" her hair; she was flushed at the adventure; she had never looked so well.

They started. Lulu, falling in with Monona, heard for the first time in her life, the step of the pursuing male, choosing to walk beside her and the little girl. Oh, would Ina like that? And what did Lulu care what Ina liked? Monona, making a silly, semi-articulate observation, was enchanted to have Lulu burst into laughter and squeeze her hand.

Di contributed her bright presence, and Bobby Larkin appeared from nowhere, running, with a gigantic bag of fruit.

"Bullylujah!" he shouted, and Lulu could have shouted with him.

She sought for some utterance. She wanted to talk with Ninian.

"I do hope we've brought sandwiches enough," was all that she could get to say.

They chose a spot, that is to say Dwight Herbert chose a spot, across the river and up the shore where there was at that season a strip of warm beach. Dwight Herbert declared himself the builder of incomparable fires, and made a bad smudge. Ninian, who was a camper neither by birth nor by adoption, kept offering brightly to help, could think of nothing to do, and presently, bethinking himself of skipping stones, went and tried to skip them on the flowing river. Ina cut her hand opening the condensed milk and was obliged to sit under a tree and nurse the wound. Monona spilled all the salt and sought diligently to recover it. So Lulu did all the work. As for Di and Bobby, they had taken the pail and gone for water, discouraging Monona from accompanying them, discouraging her to the point of tears. But the two were gone for so long that on their return Dwight was hungry and cross and majestic.

"Those who disregard the comfort of other people," he enunciated, "can not expect consideration for themselves in the future."

He did not say on what ethical tenet this dictum was based, but he delivered it with extreme authority. Ina caught her lower lip with her teeth, dipped her head, and looked at Di. And Monona laughed like a little demon.

As soon as Lulu had all in readiness, and cold corned beef and salad had begun their orderly progression, Dwight became the immemorial dweller in green fastnesses. He began:

"This is ideal. I tell you, people don't half know life if they don't get out and eat in the open. It's better than any tonic at a dollar the bottle. Nature's tonic—eh? Free as the air. Look at that sky. See that water. Could anything be more pleasant?"

He smiled at his wife. This man's face was glowing with simple pleasure. He loved the out-of-doors with a love which could not explain itself. But he now lost a definite climax when his wife's comment was heard to be:

"Monona! Now it's all over both ruffles. And mamma does try so hard. . . ."

After supper some boys arrived with a boat which they beached, and Dwight, with enthusiasm, gave the boys ten cents for a half hour's use of that boat and invited to the waters his wife, his brother and his younger daughter. Ina was timid—not because she was afraid but because she was congenitally timid—with her this was not a belief or an emotion, it was a disease.

"Dwight darling, are you sure there's no danger?"

Why, none. None in the world. Whoever heard of drowning in a river.

"But you're not so very used—"

Oh, wasn't he? Who was it that had lived in a boat throughout youth if not he?

Ninian refused out-of-hand, lighted a cigar, and sat on a log in a permanent fashion. Ina's plump figure was fitted in the stern, the child Monona affixed, and the boat put off, bow well out of water. On this pleasure ride the face of the wife was as the face of the damned. It was true that she revered her husband's opinions above those of all other men. In politics, in science, in religion, in dentistry she looked up to his dicta as to revelation. And was he not a magistrate? But let him take oars in hand, or shake lines or a whip above the back of any horse, and this woman would trust any other woman's husband by preference. It was a phenomenon.

Lulu was making the work last, so that she should be out of everybody's way. When the boat put off without Ninian, she felt a kind of terror and wished that he had gone. He had sat down near her, and she pretended not to see. At last Lulu understood that Ninian was deliberately choosing to remain with her. The languor of his bulk after the evening meal made no explanation for Lulu. She asked for no explanation. He had stayed.

And they were alone. For Di, on a pretext of examining the flocks and herds, was leading Bobby away to the pastures, a little at a time.

The sun, now fallen, had left an even, waxen sky. Leaves and ferns appeared drenched with the light just withdrawn. The hush, the warmth, the colour, were charged with some influence. The air of the time communicated itself to Lulu as intense and quiet happiness. She had not yet felt quiet with Ninian. For the first time her blind excitement in his presence ceased, and she felt curiously accustomed to him. To him the air of the time imparted itself in a deepening of his facile sympathy.

"Do you know something?" he began. "I think you have it pretty hard around here."

"I?" Lulu was genuinely astonished.

"Yes, sir. Do you have to work like this all the time? I guess you won't mind my asking."

"Well, I ought to work. I have a home with them. Mother too."

"Yes, but glory. You ought to have some kind of a life of your own. You want it, too. You told me you did—that first day."

She was silent. Again he was investing her with a longing which she had never really had, until he had planted that longing. She had wanted she knew not what. Now she accepted the dim, the romantic interest of this rôle.

"I guess you don't see how it seems," he said, "to me, coming along—a stranger so. I don't like it."

He frowned, regarded the river, flicked away ashes, his diamond obediently shining. Lulu's look, her head drooping, had the liquid air of the look of a young girl. For the first time in her life she was feeling her helplessness. It intoxicated her.

"They're very good to me," she said.

He turned. "Do you know why you think that? Because you've never had anybody really good to you. That's why."

"But they treat me good."

"They make a slave of you. Regular slave." He puffed, frowning. "Damned shame, *I* call it," he said.

Her loyalty stirred Lulu. "We have our whole living—"

"And you earn it. I been watching you since I been here. Don't you ever go anywheres?"

She said: "This is the first place in—in years."

"Lord. Don't you want to? Of course you do!"

"Not so much places like this—"

"I see. What you want is to get away—like you'd ought to." He regarded her. "You've been a blamed fine-looking woman," he said.

She did not flush, but that faint, unsuspected Lulu spoke for her:

"You must have been a good-looking man once yourself."

His laugh went ringing across the water. "You're pretty good," he said. He regarded her approvingly. "I don't see how you do it," he mused, "blamed if I do."

"How I do what?"

"Why come back, quick like that, with what you say."

Lulu's heart was beating painfully. The effort to hold her own in talk like this was terrifying. She had never talked in this fashion to any one. It was as if some matter of life or death hung on her ability to speak an alien tongue. And yet, when she was most at loss, that other Lulu, whom she had never known anything about, seemed suddenly to speak for her. As now:

"It's my grand education," she said.

She sat humped on the log, her beautiful hair shining in the light of the warm sky. She had thrown off her hat and the linen duster, and was in her blue gingham gown against the sky and leaves. But she sat stiffly, her feet carefully covered, her hands ill at ease, her eyes rather piteous in their hope somehow to hold her vague own. Yet from her came these sufficient, insouciant replies.

"Education," he said laughing heartily. "That's mine, too." He spoke a creed. "I ain't never had it and I ain't never missed it."

"Most folks are happy without an education," said Lulu.

"You're not very happy, though."

"Oh, no," she said.

"Well, sir," said Ninian, "I'll tell you what we'll do. While I'm here I'm going to take you and Ina and Dwight up to the city."

"To the city?"

"To a show. Dinner and a show. I'll give you *one* good time."

"Oh!" Lulu leaned forward. "Ina and Dwight go sometimes. I never been."

"Well, just you come with me. I'll look up what's good. You tell me just what you like to eat, and we'll get it—"

She said: "I haven't had anything to eat in years that I haven't cooked myself."

He planned for that time to come, and Lulu listened as one intensely experiencing every word that he uttered. Yet it was not in that future merry-making that she found her joy, but in the consciousness that he—some one—any one—was planning like this for her.

Meanwhile Di and Bobby had rounded the corner by an old hop-house and kept on down the levee. Now that the presence of the others was withdrawn, the two looked about them differently and began themselves to give off an influence instead of being pressed upon by overpowering personalities. Frogs were chorusing in the near swamp, and Bobby wanted one. He was off after it. But Di eventually drew him back, reluctant, frogless. He entered upon an exhaustive account of the use of frogs for bait, and as he talked he constantly flung stones. Di grew restless. There was, she had found, a certain amount of this to be gone through before Bobby would focus on the personal. At length she was obliged to say, "Like me to-day?" And then he entered upon personal talk with the same zest with which he had discussed bait.

"Bobby," said Di, "sometimes I think we might be married, and not wait for any old money."

They had now come that far. It was partly an authentic attraction, grown from out the old repulsion, and partly it was that they both—and especially Di—so much wanted the experiences of attraction that they assumed its ways. And then each cared enough to assume the pretty rôle required by the other, and by the occasion, and by the air of the time.

"Would you?" asked Bobby—but in the subjunctive.

She said: "Yes. I will."

"It would mean running away, wouldn't it?" said Bobby, still subjunctive.

"I suppose so. Mamma and papa are so unreasonable."

"Di," said Bobby, "I don't believe you could ever be happy with me."

"The idea! I can too. You're going to be a great man—you know you are."

Bobby was silent. Of course he knew it—but he passed it over.

"Wouldn't it be fun to elope and surprise the whole school?" said Di, sparkling.

Bobby grinned appreciatively. He was good to look at, with his big frame, his head of rough dark hair, the sky warm upon his clear skin and full mouth. Di suddenly announced that she would be willing to elope *now*.

"I've planned eloping lots of times," she said ambiguously.

It flashed across the mind of Bobby that in these plans of hers he may not always have been the principal, and he could not be sure . . . But she talked in nothings, and he answered her so.

Soft cries sounded in the centre of the stream. The boat, well out of the strong current, was seen to have its oars shipped; and there sat Dwight Herbert gently rocking the boat. Dwight Herbert would.

"Bertie, Bertie—please!" you heard his Ina say.

Monona began to cry, and her father was irritated, felt that it would be ignominious to desist, and did not know that he felt this. But he knew that he was annoyed, and he took refuge in this, and picked up the oars with: "Some folks never can enjoy anything without spoiling it."

"That's what I was thinking," said Ina, with a flash of anger.

They glided toward the shore in a huff. Monona found that she enjoyed crying across the water and kept it up. It was almost as good as an echo. Ina, stepping safe to the sands, cried ungratefully that this was the last time that she would ever, ever go with her husband anywhere. Ever. Dwight Herbert, recovering, gauged the moment to require of him humour, and observed that his wedded wife was as skittish as a colt. Ina kept silence, head poised so that her full little chin showed double. Monona, who had previously hidden a cooky in her frock, now remembered it and crunched sidewise, the eyes ruminant.

Moving toward them, with Di, Bobby was suddenly overtaken by the sense of disliking them all. He never had liked Dwight Herbert, his employer. Mrs. Deacon seemed to him so overwhelmingly mature that he had no idea how to treat her. And the child Monona he would like to roll in the river. Even Di . . . He fell silent, was silent on the walk home which was the signal for Di to tease him steadily. The little being was afraid of silence. It was too vast for her. She was like a butterfly in a dome.

But against that background of ruined occasion, Lulu walked homeward beside Ninian. And all that night, beside her mother who groaned in her sleep, Lulu lay tense and awake. He had walked home with her. He had told Ina and Herbert about going to the city. What did it mean? Suppose . . . oh no; oh no!

"Either lay still or get up and set up," Mrs. Bett directed her at length.

IV

July

When, on a warm evening a fortnight later, Lulu descended the stairs dressed for her incredible trip to the city, she wore the white waist which she had often thought they would "use" for her if she died. And really, the waist looked as if it had been planned for the purpose, and its wide, upstanding plaited lace at throat and wrist made her neck look thinner, her forearm sharp and veined. Her hair she had "crimped" and parted in the middle, puffed high—it was so that hair had been worn in Lulu's girlhood.

"Well!" said Ina, when she saw this coiffure, and frankly examined it, head well back, tongue meditatively teasing at her lower lip.

For travel Lulu was again wearing Ina's linen duster—the old one.

Ninian appeared, in a sack coat—and his diamond. His distinctly convex face, its thick, rosy flesh, thick mouth and cleft chin gave Lulu once more that bold sense of looking—not at him, for then she was shy and averted her eyes—but at his photograph at which she could gaze as much as she would. She looked up at him openly, fell in step beside him. Was he not taking her to the city? Ina and Dwight themselves were going because she, Lulu, had brought about this party.

"Act as good as you look, Lulie," Mrs. Bett called after them. She gave no instructions to Ina who was married and able to shine in her conduct, it seemed.

Dwight was cross. On the way to the station he might have been heard to take it up again, whatever it was, and his Ina unmistakably said: "Well, now don't keep it going all the way there"; and turned back to the others with some elaborate comment about the dust, thus cutting off her so-called lord from his legitimate retort. A mean advantage.

The city was two hours' distant, and they were to spend the night. On the train, in the double seat, Ninian beside her among the bags, Lulu sat in the simple consciousness that the people all knew that she too had been chosen. A man and a woman were opposite, with their little boy between them. Lulu felt this woman's superiority of experience over her own, and smiled at her from a world of fellowship. But the woman lifted her eyebrows and stared and turned away, with slow and insolent winking.

Ninian had a boyish pride in his knowledge of places to eat in many cities—as if he were leading certain of the tribe to a deer-run in a strange wood. Ninian took his party to a downtown café, then popular among business and newspaper men. The place was below the sidewalk, was reached by a dozen marble steps, and the odour of its griddle-cakes took the air of the street. Ninian made a great show of selecting a table, changed once, called the waiter "my man" and rubbed soft hands on "What do you say? Shall it be lobster?" He ordered the dinner, instructing the waiter with painstaking gruffness.

"Not that they can touch *your* cooking here, Miss Lulu," he said, settling himself to wait, and crumbling a crust.

Dwight, expanding a bit in the aura of the food, observed that Lulu was a regular chef, that was what Lulu was. He still would not look at his wife, who now remarked:

"Sheff, Dwightie. Not cheff."

This was a mean advantage, which he pretended not to hear—another mean advantage.

"Ina," said Lulu, "your hat's just a little mite—no, over the other way."

"Was there anything to prevent your speaking of that before?" Ina inquired acidly.

"I started to and then somebody always said something," said Lulu humbly.

Nothing could so much as cloud Lulu's hour. She was proof against any shadow.

"Say, but you look tremendous to-night," Dwight observed to her.

Understanding perfectly that this was said to tease his wife, Lulu yet flushed with pleasure. She saw two women watching, and she thought: "They're feeling sorry for Ina—nobody talking to her." She laughed at everything that the men said. She passionately wanted to talk herself. "How many folks keep going past," she said, many times.

At length, having noted the details of all the clothes in range, Ina's isolation palled upon her and she set herself to take Ninian's attention. She therefore talked with him about himself.

"Curious you've never married, Nin," she said.

"Don't say it like that," he begged. "I might yet."

Ina laughed enjoyably. "Yes, you might!" she met this.

"She wants everybody to get married, but she wishes I hadn't," Dwight threw in with exceeding rancour.

They developed this theme exhaustively, Dwight usually speaking in the third person and always with his shoulder turned a bit from his wife. It was inconceivable, the gusto with which they proceeded. Ina had assumed for the purpose an air distrait, casual, attentive to the scene about them. But gradually her cheeks began to burn.

"She'll cry," Lulu thought in alarm, and said at random: "Ina, that hat is so pretty—ever so much prettier than the old one." But Ina said frostily that she never saw anything the matter with the old one.

"Let us talk," said Ninian low, to Lulu. "Then they'll simmer down."

He went on, in an undertone, about nothing in particular. Lulu hardly heard what he said, it was so pleasant to have him talking to her in this confidential fashion; and she was pleasantly aware that his manner was open to misinterpretation.

In the nick of time, the lobster was served.

Dinner and the play—the show, as Ninian called it. This show was "Peter Pan," chosen by Ninian because the seats cost the most of those at any theatre. It was almost indecent to see how Dwight Herbert, the immortal soul, had warmed and melted at these contacts. By the time that all was over, and they were at the hotel for supper, such was his pleasurable excitation that he was once more playful, teasing, once more the irrepressible. But now his

Ina was to be won back, made it evident that she was not one lightly to overlook, and a fine firmness sat upon the little doubling chin.

They discussed the play. Not one of them had understood the story. The dog-kennel part—wasn't that the queerest thing? Nothing to do with the rest of the play.

"I was for the pirates. The one with the hook—he was my style," said Dwight.

"Well, there it is again," Ina cried. "They didn't belong to the real play, either."

"Oh, well," Ninian said, "they have to put in parts, I suppose, to catch everybody. Instead of a song and dance, they do that."

"And I didn't understand," said Ina, "why they all clapped when the principal character ran down front and said something to the audience that time. But they all did."

Ninian thought this might have been out of compliment. Ina wished that Monona might have seen, confessed that the last part was so pretty that she herself would not look; and into Ina's eyes came their loveliest light.

Lulu sat there, hearing the talk about the play. "Why couldn't I have said that?" she thought as the others spoke. All that they said seemed to her apropos, but she could think of nothing to add. The evening had been to her a light from heaven—how could she find anything to say? She sat in a daze of happiness, her mind hardly operative, her look moving from one to another. At last Ninian looked at her.

"Sure you liked it, Miss Lulu?"

"Oh, yes! I think they all took their parts real well."

It was not enough. She looked at them appealingly, knowing that she had not said enough.

"You could hear everything they said," she added. "It was—" she dwindled to silence.

Dwight Herbert savoured his rarebit with a great show of long wrinkled dimples.

"Excellent sauces they make here—excellent," he said, with the frown of an epicure. "A tiny wee bit more Athabasca," he added, and they all laughed and told him that Athabasca was a lake, of course. Of course he meant Tabasco, Ina said. Their entertainment and their talk was of this sort, for an hour.

"Well, now," said Dwight Herbert when it was finished, "somebody dance on the table."

"Dwightie!"

"Got to amuse ourselves somehow. Come, liven up. They'll begin to read the funeral service over us."

"Why not say the wedding service?" asked Ninian.

In the mention of wedlock there was always something stimulating to Dwight, something of overwhelming humour. He shouted a derisive endorsement of this proposal.

"I shouldn't object," said Ninian. "Should you, Miss Lulu?"

Lulu now burned the slow red of her torture. They were all looking at her. She made an anguished effort to defend herself.

"I don't know it," she said, "so I can't say it."

Ninian leaned toward her.

"I, Ninian, take thee, Lulu, to be my wedded wife," he pronounced. "That's the way it goes!"

"Lulu daren't say it!" cried Dwight. He laughed so loudly that those at the near tables turned. And, from the fastness of her wifehood and motherhood, Ina laughed. Really, it was ridiculous to think of Lulu that way. . . .

Ninian laughed too. "Course she don't dare say it," he challenged.

From within Lulu, that strange Lulu, that other Lulu who sometimes fought her battles, suddenly spoke out:

"I, Lulu, take thee, Ninian, to be my wedded husband."

"You will?" Ninian cried.

"I will," she said, laughing tremulously, to prove that she too could join in, could be as merry as the rest.

"And I will. There, by Jove, now have we entertained you, or haven't we?" Ninian laughed and pounded his soft fist on the table.

"Oh, say, honestly!" Ina was shocked. "I don't think you ought to—holy things—what's the *matter*, Dwightie?"

Dwight Herbert Deacon's eyes were staring and his face was scarlet.

"Say, by George," he said, "a civil wedding is binding in this state."

"A civil wedding? Oh, well—" Ninian dismissed it.

"But I," said Dwight, "happen to be a magistrate."

They looked at one another foolishly. Dwight sprang up with the indeterminate idea of inquiring something of some one, circled about and returned. Ina had taken his chair and sat clasping Lulu's hand. Ninian continued to laugh.

"I never saw one done so offhand," said Dwight. "But what you've said is all you have to say according to law. And there don't have to be witnesses . . . say!" he said, and sat down again.

Above that shroud-like plaited lace, the veins of Lulu's throat showed dark as she swallowed, cleared her throat, swallowed again.

"Don't you let Dwight scare you," she besought Ninian.

"Scare me!" cried Ninian. "Why, I think it's a good job done, if you ask me."

Lulu's eyes flew to his face. As he laughed, he was looking at her, and now he nodded and shut and opened his eyes several times very fast. Their points of light flickered. With a pang of wonder which pierced her and left her shaken, Lulu looked. His eyes continued to meet her own. It was exactly like looking at his photograph.

Dwight had recovered his authentic air.

"Oh, well," he said, "we can inquire at our leisure. If it is necessary, I should say we can have it set aside quietly up here in the city—no one'll be the wiser."

"Set aside nothing!" said Ninian. "I'd like to see it stand."

"Are you serious, Nin?"

"Sure I'm serious."

Ina jerked gently at her sister's arm.

"Lulu! You hear him? What you going to say to that?"

Lulu shook her head. "He isn't in earnest," she said.

"I am in earnest—hope to die," Ninian declared. He was on two legs of his chair and was slightly tilting, so that the effect of his earnestness was impaired. But he was obviously in earnest.

They were looking at Lulu again. And now she looked at Ninian, and there was something terrible in that look which tried to ask him, alone, about this thing.

Dwight exploded. "There was a fellow I know there in the theatre," he cried. "I'll get him on the line. He could tell me if there's any way—" and was off.

Ina inexplicably began touching away tears. "Oh," she said, "what will mamma say?"

Lulu hardly heard her. Mrs. Bett was incalculably distant.

"You sure?" Lulu said low to Ninian.

For the first time, something in her exceeding isolation really touched him.

"Say," he said, "you come on with me. We'll have it done over again somewhere, if you say so."

"Oh," said Lulu, "if I thought—"

He leaned and patted her hand.

"Good girl," he said.

They sat silent, Ninian padding on the cloth with the flat of his plump hands.

Dwight returned. "It's a go all right," he said. He sat down, laughed weakly, rubbed at his face. "You two are tied as tight as the church could tie you."

"Good enough," said Ninian. "Eh, Lulu?"

"It's—it's all right, I guess," Lulu said.

"Well, I'll be dished," said Dwight.

"Sister!" said Ina.

Ninian meditated, his lips set tight and high. It is impossible to trace the processes of this man. Perhaps they were all compact of the devil-may-care attitude engendered in any persistent traveller. Perhaps the incomparable cookery of Lulu played its part.

"I was going to make a trip south this month," he said, "on my way home from here. Suppose we get married again by somebody or other, and start right off. You'd like that, wouldn't you—going South?"

"Yes," said Lulu only.

"It's July," said Ina, with her sense of fitness, but no one heard.

It was arranged that their trunks should follow them—Ina would see to that, though she was scandalised that they were not first to return to Warbleton for the blessing of Mrs. Bett.

"Mamma won't mind," said Lulu. "Mamma can't stand a fuss any more."

They left the table. The men and women still sitting at the

other tables saw nothing unusual about these four, indifferently dressed, indifferently conditioned. The hotel orchestra, playing ragtime in deafening concord, made Lulu's wedding march.

It was still early next day—a hot Sunday—when Ina and Dwight reached home. Mrs. Bett was standing on the porch.

"Where's Lulie?" asked Mrs. Bett.

They told.

Mrs. Bett took it in, a bit at a time. Her pale eyes searched their faces, she shook her head, heard it again, grasped it. Her first question was:

"Who's going to do your work?"

Ina had thought of that, and this was manifest.

"Oh," she said, "you and I'll have to manage."

Mrs. Bett meditated, frowning.

"I left the bacon for her to cook for your breakfasts," she said. "I can't cook bacon fit to eat. Neither can you."

"We've had our breakfasts," Ina escaped from this dilemma.

"Had it up in the city, on expense?"

"Well, we didn't have much."

In Mrs. Bett's eyes tears gathered, but they were not for Lulu.

"I should think," she said, "I should think Lulie might have had a little more gratitude to her than this."

On their way to church Ina and Dwight encountered Di, who had left the house some time earlier, stepping sedately to church in company with Bobby Larkin. Di was in white, and her face was the face of an angel, so young, so questioning, so utterly devoid of her sophistication.

"That child," said Ina, "*must* not see so much of that Larkin boy. She's just a little, little girl."

"Of course she mustn't," said Dwight sharply, "and if *I* was her mother—"

"Oh stop that!" said Ina, sotto voce, at the church steps.

To every one with whom they spoke in the aisle after church, Ina announced their news: Had they heard? Lulu married Dwight's brother Ninian in the city yesterday. Oh, sudden, yes! And ro*man*tic . . . spoken with that upward inflection to which Ina was a prey.

V

August

Mrs. Bett had been having a "tantrim," brought on by nothing definable. Abruptly as she and Ina were getting supper, Mrs. Bett had fallen silent, had in fact refused to reply when addressed. When all was ready and Dwight was entering, hair wetly brushed, she had withdrawn from the room and closed her bedroom door until it echoed.

"She's got one again," said Ina, grieving. "Dwight, you go."

He went, showing no sign of annoyance, and stood outside his mother-in-law's door and knocked.

No answer.

"Mother, come and have some supper."

No answer.

"Looks to me like your muffins was just about the best ever."

No answer.

"Come on—I had something funny to tell you and Ina."

He retreated, knowing nothing of the admirable control exercised by this woman for her own passionate satisfaction in sending him away unsatisfied. He showed nothing but anxious concern, touched with regret, at his failure. Ina, too, returned from that door discomfited. Dwight made a gallant effort to retrieve the fallen fortunes of their evening meal, and turned upon Di, who had just entered, and with exceeding facetiousness inquired how Bobby was.

Di looked hunted. She could never tell whether her parents were going to tease her about Bobby, or rebuke her for being seen with him. It depended on mood, and this mood Di had not the experience to gauge. She now groped for some neutral fact, and mentioned that he was going to take her and Jenny for ice cream that night.

Ina's irritation found just expression in her office of motherhood.

"I won't have you downtown in the evening," she said.

"But you let me go last night."

"All the better reason why you should not go to-night."

"I tell you," cried Dwight. "Why not all walk down? Why not all have ice cream . . ." He was all gentleness and propitiation, the reconciling element in his home.

"Me too?" Monona's ardent hope, her terrible fear were in her eyebrows, her parted lips.

"You too, certainly." Dwight could not do enough for every one.

Monona clapped her hands. "Goody! Goody! Last time you wouldn't let me go."

"That's why papa's going to take you this time," Ina said.

These ethical balances having been nicely struck, Ina proposed another:

"But," she said, "but, you must eat more supper or you can *not* go."

"I don't want any more." Monona's look was honest and piteous.

"Makes no difference. You must eat or you'll get sick."

"No!"

"Very well, then. No ice cream soda for such a little girl."

Monona began to cry quietly. But she passed her plate. She ate, chewing high, and slowly.

"See? She can eat if she will eat," Ina said to Dwight. "The only trouble is, she will *not* take the time."

"She don't put her mind on her meals," Dwight Herbert diagnosed it. "Oh, bigger bites than that!" he encouraged his little daughter.

Di's mind had been proceeding along its own paths.

"Are you going to take Jenny and Bobby too?" she inquired.

"Certainly. The whole party."

"Bobby'll want to pay for Jenny and I."

"Me, darling," said Ina patiently, punctiliously—and less punctiliously added: "Nonsense. This is going to be papa's little party."

"But we had the engagement with Bobby. It was an engagement."

"Well," said Ina, "I think we'll just set that aside—that important engagement. I think we just will."

"Papa! Bobby'll want to be the one to pay for Jenny and I—"

"Di!" Ina's voice dominated all. "Will you be more careful of your grammar or shall I speak to you again?"

"Well, I'd rather use bad grammar than—than—than—" she looked resentfully at her mother, her father. Their moral defection was evident to her, but it was indefinable. They told her that she ought to be ashamed when papa wanted to give them all a treat. She sat silent, frowning, put-upon.

"Look, mamma!" cried Monona, swallowing a third of an egg at one impulse. Ina saw only the empty plate.

"Mamma's nice little girl!" cried she, shining upon her child.

The rules of the ordinary sports of the playground, scrupulously applied, would have clarified the ethical atmosphere of this little family. But there was no one to apply them.

When Di and Monona had been excused, Dwight asked:

"Nothing new from the bride and groom?"

"No. And, Dwight, it's been a week since the last."

"See—where were they then?"

He knew perfectly well that they were in Savannah, Georgia, but Ina played his game, told him, and retold bits that the letter had said.

"I don't understand," she added, "why they should go straight to Oregon without coming here first."

Dwight hazarded that Nin probably had to get back, and shone pleasantly in the reflected importance of a brother filled with affairs.

"I don't know what to make of Lulu's letters," Ina proceeded. "They're so—so—"

"You haven't had but two, have you?"

"That's all—well, of course it's only been a month. But both letters have been so—"

Ina was never really articulate. Whatever corner of her brain had the blood in it at the moment seemed to be operative, and she let the matter go at that.

"I don't think it's fair to mamma—going off that way. Leaving her own mother. Why, she may never see mamma again—" Ina's breath caught. Into her face came something of the lovely tenderness with which she sometimes looked at Monona and Di. She sprang up. She had forgotten to put some supper to warm for mamma. The lovely light was still in her face as she bustled about against the time of mamma's recovery from her tantrim. Dwight's face was like this when he spoke of his foster-mother. In both these beings there was something which functioned as pure love.

Mamma had recovered and was eating cold scrambled eggs on the corner of the kitchen table when the ice cream soda party was ready to set out. Dwight threw her a casual "Better come, too, Mother Bett," but she shook her head. She wished to go, wished it with violence, but she contrived to give to her arbitrary refusal a quality of contempt. When Jenny arrived with Bobby, she had brought a sheaf of gladioli for Mrs. Bett, and took them to her in the kitchen, and as she laid the flowers beside her, the young girl stopped and kissed her. "You little darling!" cried Mrs. Bett, and clung to her, her lifted eyes lit by something intense and living. But when the ice cream party had set off at last, Mrs. Bett left her supper, gathered up the flowers, and crossed the lawn to the old cripple, Grandma Gates.

"Inie sha'n't have 'em," the old woman thought.

And then it was quite beautiful to watch her with Grandma Gates, whom she tended and petted, to whose complainings she listened, and to whom she tried to tell the small events of her day. When her neighbour had gone, Grandma Gates said that it was as good as a dose of medicine to have her come in.

Mrs. Bett sat on the porch restored and pleasant when the family returned. Di and Bobby had walked home with Jenny.

"Look here," said Dwight Herbert, "who is it sits home and has *ice* cream put in her lap, like a queen?"

"Vanilly or chocolate?" Mrs. Bett demanded.

"Chocolate, mamma!" Ina cried, with the breeze in her voice.

"Vanilly sets better," Mrs. Bett said.

They sat with her on the porch while she ate. Ina rocked on a creaking board. Dwight swung a leg over the railing. Monona sat pulling her skirt over her feet, and humming all on one note. There was no moon, but the warm dusk had a quality of transparency as if it were lit in all its particles.

The gate opened, and some one came up the walk. They looked, and it was Lulu.

"Well, if it ain't Miss Lulu Bett!" Dwight cried involuntarily, and Ina cried out something.

"How did you know?" Lulu asked.

"Know! Know what?"

"That it ain't Lulu Deacon. Hello, mamma."

She passed the others, and kissed her mother.

"Say," said Mrs. Bett placidly. "And I just ate up the last spoonful o' cream."

"Ain't Lulu Deacon!" Ina's voice rose and swelled richly. "What you talking?"

"Didn't he write to you?" Lulu asked.

"Not a word." Dwight answered this. "All we've had we had from you—the last from Savannah, Georgia."

"Savannah, Georgia," said Lulu, and laughed.

They could see that she was dressed well, in dark red cloth, with a little tilting hat and a drooping veil. She did not seem in any wise upset, nor, save for that nervous laughter, did she show her excitement.

"Well, but he's here with you, isn't he?" Dwight demanded. "Isn't he here? Where is he?"

"Must be 'most to Oregon by this time," Lulu said.

"Oregon!"

"You see," said Lulu, "he had another wife."

"Why, he had not!" exclaimed Dwight absurdly.

"Yes. He hasn't seen her for fifteen years and he thinks she's dead. But he isn't sure."

"Nonsense," said Dwight. "Why, of course she's dead if he thinks so."

"I had to be sure," said Lulu.

At first dumb before this, Ina now cried out: "Monona! Go upstairs to bed at once."

"It's only quarter to," said Monona, with assurance.

"Do as mamma tells you."

"But—"

"Monona!"

She went, kissing them all good-night and taking her time about it. Everything was suspended while she kissed them and departed, walking slowly backward.

"Married?" said Mrs. Bett with tardy apprehension. "Lulie, was your husband married?"

"Yes," Lulu said, "my husband was married, mother."

"Mercy," said Ina. "Think of anything like that in our family."

"Well, go on—go on!" Dwight cried. "Tell us about it."

Lulu spoke in a monotone, with her old manner of hesitation:

"We were going to Oregon. First down to New Orleans and then out to California and up the coast." On this she paused and sighed. "Well, then at Savannah, Georgia, he said he thought I better know, first. So he told me."

"Yes—well, what did he *say*?" Dwight demanded irritably.

"Cora Waters," said Lulu. "Cora Waters. She married him down in San Diego, eighteen years ago. She went to South America with him."

"Well, he never let us know of it, if she did," said Dwight.

"No. She married him just before he went. Then in South America, after two years, she ran away again. That's all he knows."

"That's a pretty story," said Dwight contemptuously.

"He says if she'd been alive, she'd been after him for a divorce. And she never has been, so he thinks she must be dead. The trouble is," Lulu said again, "he wasn't sure. And I had to be sure."

"Well, but mercy," said Ina, "couldn't he find out now?"

"It might take a long time," said Lulu simply, "and I didn't want to stay and not know."

"Well, then, why didn't he say so here?" Ina's indignation mounted.

"He would have. But you know how sudden everything was. He said he thought about telling us right there in the restaurant, but of course that'd been hard—wouldn't it? And then he felt so sure she was dead."

"Why did he tell you at all, then?" demanded Ina, whose processes were simple.

"Yes. Well! Why indeed?" Dwight Herbert brought out these words with a curious emphasis.

"I thought that, just at first," Lulu said, "but only just at first. Of course that wouldn't have been right. And then, you see, he gave me my choice."

"Gave you your choice?" Dwight echoed.

"Yes. About going on and taking the chances. He gave me my choice when he told me, there in Savannah, Georgia."

"What made him conclude, by then, that you ought to be told?" Dwight asked.

"Why, he'd got to thinking about it," she answered.

A silence fell. Lulu sat looking out toward the street.

"The only thing," she said, "as long as it happened, I kind of wish he hadn't told me till we got to Oregon."

"Lulu!" said Ina. Ina began to cry. "You poor thing!" she said.

Her tears were a signal to Mrs. Bett, who had been striving to understand all. Now she too wept, tossing up her hands and rocking her body. Her saucer and spoon clattered on her knee.

"He felt bad too," Lulu said.

"He!" said Dwight. "He must have."

"It's you," Ina sobbed. "It's you. *My* sister!"

"Well," said Lulu, "but I never thought of it making you both feel bad, or I wouldn't have come home. I knew," she added, "it'd make Dwight feel bad. I mean, it was his brother—"

"Thank goodness," Ina broke in, "nobody need know about it."

Lulu regarded her, without change.

"Oh, yes," she said in her monotone. "People will have to know."

"I do not see the necessity." Dwight's voice was an edge. Then too he said "do not," always with Dwight betokening the finalities.

"Why, what would they think?" Lulu asked, troubled.

"What difference does it make what they think?"

"Why," said Lulu slowly, "I shouldn't like—you see they might—why, Dwight, I think we'll have to tell them."

"You do! You think the disgrace of bigamy in this family is something the whole town will have to know about?"

Lulu looked at him with parted lips.

"Say," she said, "I never thought about it being that."

Dwight laughed. "What did you think it was? And whose disgrace is it, pray?"

"Ninian's," said Lulu.

"Ninian's! Well, he's gone. But you're here. And I'm here. Folks'll feel sorry for you. But the disgrace—that'd reflect on me. See?"

"But if we don't tell, what'll they think then?"

Said Dwight: "They'll think what they always think when a wife leaves her husband. They'll think you couldn't get along. That's all."

"I should hate that," said Lulu.

"Well, I should hate the other, let me tell you."

"Dwight, Dwight," said Ina. "Let's go in the house. I'm afraid they'll hear—"

As they rose, Mrs. Bett plucked at her returned daughter's sleeve.

"Lulie," she said, "was his other wife—was she *there*?"

"No, no, mother. She wasn't there."

Mrs. Bett's lips moved, repeating the words. "Then that ain't so bad," she said. "I was afraid maybe she turned you out."

"No," Lulu said, "it wasn't that bad, mother."

Mrs. Bett brightened. In little matters, she quarrelled and resented, but the large issues left her blank.

Through some indeterminate sense of the importance due this crisis, the Deacons entered their parlour. Dwight lighted that high, central burner and faced about, saying:

"In fact, I simply will not have it, Lulu! You expect, I take it, to make your home with us in the future, on the old terms."

"Well—"

"I mean, did Ninian give you any money?"

"No. He didn't give me any money—only enough to get home on. And I kept my suit—why!" she flung her head back, "I wouldn't have taken any money!"

"That means," said Dwight, "that you will have to continue to live here—on the old terms, and of course I'm quite willing that you should. Let me tell you, however, that this is on condition—on condition that this disgraceful business is kept to ourselves."

She made no attempt to combat him now. She looked back at him, quivering, and in a great surprise, but she said nothing.

"Truly, Lulu," said Ina, "wouldn't that be best? They'll talk anyway. But this way they'll only talk about you, and the other way it'd be about all of us."

Lulu said only: "But the other way would be the truth."

Dwight's eyes narrowed: "My dear Lulu," he said, "are you *sure* of that?"

"Sure?"

"Yes. Did he give you any proofs?"

"Proofs?"

"Letters—documents of any sort? Any sort of assurance that he was speaking the truth?"

"Why, no," said Lulu. "Proofs—no. He told me."

"He told you!"

"Why, that was hard enough to have to do. It was terrible for him to have to do. What proofs—" She stopped, puzzled.

"Didn't it occur to you," said Dwight, "that he might have told you that because he didn't want to have to go on with it?"

As she met his look, some power seemed to go from Lulu. She sat down, looked weakly at them, and within her closed lips her jaw was slightly fallen. She said nothing. And seeing on her skirt a spot of dust she began to rub at that.

"Why, Dwight!" Ina cried, and moved to her sister's side.

"I may as well tell you," he said, "that I myself have no idea that Ninian told you the truth. He was always imagining things—you saw that. I know him pretty well—have been more or less in touch with him the whole time. In short, I haven't the least idea he was ever married before."

Lulu continued to rub at her skirt.

"I never thought of that," she said.

"Look here," Dwight went on persuasively, "hadn't you and he had some little tiff when he told you?"

"No—no! Why, not once. Why, we weren't a bit like you and Ina."

She spoke simply and from her heart and without guile.

"Evidently not," Dwight said drily.

Lulu went on: "He was very good to me. This dress—and my shoes—and my hat. And another dress, too." She found the pins and took off her hat. "He liked the red wing," she said. "I wanted black—oh, Dwight! He did tell me the truth!" It was as if the red wing had abruptly borne mute witness.

Dwight's tone now mounted. His manner, it mounted too.

"Even if it is true," said he, "I desire that you should keep silent and protect my family from this scandal. I merely mention my doubts to you for your own profit."

"My own profit!"

She said no more, but rose and moved to the door.

"Lulu—you see! With Di and all!" Ina begged. "We just couldn't have this known—even if it was so."

"You have it in your hands," said Dwight, "to repay me, Lulu, for anything that you feel I may have done for you in the past. You also have it in your hands to decide whether your home here continues. That is not a pleasant position for me to find myself in. It is distinctly unpleasant, I may say. But you see for yourself."

Lulu went on, into the passage.

"Wasn't she married when she thought she was?" Mrs. Bett cried shrilly.

"Mamma," said Ina. "Do, please, remember Monona. Yes—Dwight thinks she's married all right now—and that it's all right, all the time."

"Well, I hope so, for pity sakes," said Mrs. Bett, and left the room with her daughter.

Hearing the stir, Monona upstairs lifted her voice:

"Mamma! Come on and hear my prayers, why don't you?"

When they came downstairs next morning, Lulu had breakfast ready.

"Well!" cried Ina in her curving tone, "if this isn't like old times."

Lulu said yes, that it was like old times, and brought the bacon to the table.

"Lulu's the only one in *this* house can cook the bacon so's it'll chew," Mrs. Bett volunteered. She was wholly affable, and held contentedly to Ina's last word that Dwight thought now it was all right.

"Ho!" said Dwight. "The happy family, once more about the festive toaster." He gauged the moment to call for good cheer. Ina, too, became breezy, blithe. Monona caught their spirit and laughed, head thrown well back and gently shaken.

Di came in. She had been told that Auntie Lulu was at home, and that she, Di, wasn't to say anything to her about anything, nor anything to anybody else about Auntie Lulu being back. Under these prohibitions, which loosed a thousand speculations, Di was very nearly paralysed. She stared at her Aunt Lulu incessantly.

Not one of them had even a talent for the casual, save Lulu herself. Lulu was amazingly herself. She took her old place, assumed her old offices. When Monona declared against bacon, it was Lulu who suggested milk toast and went to make it.

"Mamma," Di whispered then, like escaping steam, "isn't Uncle Ninian coming too?"

"Hush. No. Now don't ask any more questions."

"Well, can't I tell Bobby and Jenny she's here?"

"*No.* Don't say anything at all about her."

"But, mamma. What has she done?"

"Di! Do as mamma tells you. Don't you think mamma knows best?"

Di of course did not think so, had not thought so for a long time. But now Dwight said:

"Daughter! Are you a little girl or are you our grown-up young lady?"

"I don't know," said Di reasonably, "but I think you're treating me like a little girl now."

"Shame, Di," said Ina, unabashed by the accident of reason being on the side of Di.

"I'm eighteen," Di reminded them forlornly, "and through high school."

"Then act so," boomed her father.

Baffled, thwarted, bewildered, Di went over to Jenny Plow's and there imparted understanding by the simple process of letting Jenny guess, to questions skillfully shaped.

When Dwight said, "Look at my beautiful handkerchief,"

displayed a hole, sent his Ina for a better, Lulu, with a manner of haste, addressed him:

"Dwight. It's a funny thing, but I haven't Ninian's Oregon address."

"Well?"

"Well, I wish you'd give it to me."

Dwight tightened and lifted his lips. "It would seem," he said, "that you have no real use for that particular address, Lulu."

"Yes, I have. I want it. You have it, haven't you, Dwight?"

"Certainly I have it."

"Won't you please write it down for me?" She had ready a bit of paper and a pencil stump.

"My dear Lulu, now why revive anything? Why not be sensible and leave this alone? No good can come by—"

"But why shouldn't I have his address?"

"If everything is over between you, why should you?"

"But you say he's still my husband."

Dwight flushed. "If my brother has shown his inclination as plainly as I judge that he has, it is certainly not my place to put you in touch with him again."

"You won't give it to me?"

"My dear Lulu, in all kindness—no."

His Ina came running back, bearing handkerchiefs with different coloured borders for him to choose from. He chose the initial that she had embroidered, and had not the good taste not to kiss her.

They were all on the porch that evening, when Lulu came downstairs.

"*Where* are you going?" Ina demanded, sisterly. And on hearing that Lulu had an errand, added still more sisterly; "Well, but mercy, what you so dressed up for?"

Lulu was in a thin black-and-white gown which they had never seen, and wore the tilting hat with the red wing.

"Ninian bought me this," said Lulu only.

"But, Lulu, don't you think it might be better to keep, well—out of sight for a few days?" Ina's lifted look besought her.

"Why?" Lulu asked.

"Why set people wondering till we have to?"

"They don't have to wonder, far as I'm concerned," said Lulu, and went down the walk.

Ina looked at Dwight. "She never spoke to me like that in her life before," she said.

She watched her sister's black-and-white figure going erectly down the street.

"That gives me the funniest feeling," said Ina, "as if Lulu had on clothes bought for her by some one that wasn't—that was—"

"By her husband who has left her," said Dwight sadly.

"Is that what it is, papa?" Di asked alertly. For a wonder, she was there; had been there the greater part of the day—most of the time staring, fascinated, at her Aunt Lulu.

"That's what it is, my little girl," said Dwight, and shook his head.

"Well, I think it's a shame," said Di stoutly. "And I think Uncle Ninian is a slunge."

"Di!"

"I do. And I'd be ashamed to think anything else. I'd like to tell everybody."

"There is," said Dwight, "no need for secrecy—now."

"Dwight!" said Ina—Ina's eyes always remained expressionless, but it must have been her lashes that looked so startled.

"No need whatever for secrecy," he repeated with firmness. "The truth is, Lulu's husband has tired of her and sent her home. We must face it."

"But, Dwight—how awful for Lulu . . ."

"Lulu," said Dwight, "has us to stand by her."

Lulu, walking down the main street, thought:

"Now Mis' Chambers is seeing me. Now Mis' Curtis. There's somebody behind the vines at Mis' Martin's. Here comes Mis' Grove and I've got to speak to her. . . ."

One and another and another met her, and every one cried out at her some version of:

"Lulu Bett!" Or, "W-well, it *isn't* Lulu Bett any more, is it? Well, what are you doing here? I thought . . ."

"I'm back to stay," she said.

"The idea! Well, where you hiding that handsome husband of yours? Say, but we were surprised! You're the sly one—"

"My—Mr. Deacon isn't here."

"Oh."

"No. He's West."

"Oh, I see."

Having no arts, she must needs let the conversation die like this, could invent nothing concealing or gracious on which to move away.

She went to the post-office. It was early, there were few at the post-office—with only one or two there had she to go through her examination. Then she went to the general delivery window, tense for a new ordeal.

To her relief, the face which was shown there was one strange to her, a slim youth, reading a letter of his own, and smiling.

"Excuse me," said Lulu faintly.

The youth looked up, with eyes warmed by the words on the pink paper which he held.

"Could you give me the address of Mr. Ninian Deacon?"

"Let's see—you mean Dwight Deacon, I guess?"

"No. It's his brother. He's been here. From Oregon. I thought he might have given you his address—" she dwindled away.

"Wait a minute," said the youth. "Nope. No address here. Say, why don't you send it to his brother? He'd know. Dwight Deacon, the dentist."

"I'll do that," Lulu said absurdly, and turned away.

She went back up the street, walking fast now to get away from them all. Once or twice she pretended not to see a familiar face. But when she passed the mirror in an insurance office window, she saw her reflection and at its appearance she felt surprise and pleasure.

"Well!" she thought, almost in Ina's own manner.

Abruptly her confidence rose.

Something of this confidence was still upon her when she returned. They were in the dining-room now, all save Di, who was on the porch with Bobby, and Monona, who was in bed and might be heard extravagantly singing.

Lulu sat down with her hat on. When Dwight inquired playfully, "Don't we look like company?" she did not reply. He looked at her speculatively. Where had she gone, with whom had she talked, what had she told? Ina looked at her rather fearfully. But Mrs. Bett rocked contentedly and ate cardamom seeds.

"Whom did you see?" Ina asked.

Lulu named them.

"See them to talk to?" from Dwight.

Oh, yes. They had all stopped.

"What did they say?" Ina burst out.

They had inquired for Ninian, Lulu said; and said no more.

Dwight mulled this. Lulu might have told every one of these women that cock-and-bull story with which she had come home. It might be all over town. Of course, in that case he could turn Lulu out—should do so, in fact. Still the story would be all over town.

"Dwight," said Lulu, "I want Ninian's address."

"Going to write to him!" Ina cried incredulously.

"I want to ask him for the proofs that Dwight wanted."

"My dear Lulu," Dwight said impatiently, "you are not the one to write. Have you no delicacy?"

Lulu smiled—a strange smile, originating and dying in one corner of her mouth.

"Yes," she said. "So much delicacy that I want to be sure whether I'm married or not."

Dwight cleared his throat with a movement which seemed to use his shoulders for the purpose.

"I myself will take this up with my brother," he said. "I will write to him about it."

Lulu sprang to her feet. "Write to him *now*!" she cried.

"Really," said Dwight, lifting his brows.

"Now—now!" Lulu said. She moved about, collecting writing materials from their casual lodgments on shelf and table. She set all before him and stood by him. "Write to him now," she said again.

"My dear Lulu, don't be absurd."

She said: "Ina. Help me. If it was Dwight—and they didn't know whether he had another wife, or not, and you wanted to ask him—oh, don't you see? Help me."

Ina was not yet the woman to cry for justice for its own sake, nor even to stand by another woman. She was primitive, and her instinct was to look to her own male merely.

"Well," she said, "of course. But why not let Dwight do it in his own way? Wouldn't that be better?"

She put it to her sister fairly: Now, no matter what Dwight's way was, wouldn't that be better?

"Mother!" said Lulu. She looked irresolutely toward her mother. But Mrs. Bett was eating cardamom seeds with exceeding gusto, and Lulu looked away. Caught by the gesture, Mrs. Bett voiced her grievance.

"Lulie," she said, "set down. Take off your hat, why don't you?"

Lulu turned upon Dwight a quiet face which he had never seen before.

"You write that letter to Ninian," she said, "and you make him tell you so you'll understand. *I* know he spoke the truth. But I want you to know."

"M—m," said Dwight. "And then I suppose you're going to tell it all over town—as soon as you have the proofs."

"I'm going to tell it all over town," said Lulu, "just as it is—unless you write to him now."

"Lulu!" cried Ina. "Oh, you wouldn't."

"I would," said Lulu. "I will."

Dwight was sobered. This unimagined Lulu looked capable of it. But then he sneered.

"And get turned out of this house, as you would be?"

"Dwight!" cried his Ina. "Oh, you wouldn't!"

"I would," said Dwight. "I will. Lulu knows it."

"I shall tell what I know and then leave your house anyway," said Lulu, "unless you get Ninian's word. And I want you should write him now."

"Leave your mother? And Ina?" he asked.

"Leave everything," said Lulu.

"Oh, Dwight," said Ina, "we can't get along without Lulu." She did not say in what particulars, but Dwight knew.

Dwight looked at Lulu, an upward, sidewise look, with a manner of peering out to see if she meant it. And he saw.

He shrugged, pursed his lips crookedly, rolled his head to signify the inexpressible. "Isn't that like a woman?" he demanded. He rose. "Rather than let you in for a show of temper," he said grandly, "I'd do anything."

He wrote the letter, addressed it, his hand elaborately curved in secrecy about the envelope, pocketed it.

"Ina and I'll walk down with you to mail it," said Lulu.

Dwight hesitated, frowned. His Ina watched him with consulting brows.

"I was going," said Dwight, "to propose a little stroll before bedtime." He roved about the room. "Where's my beautiful straw hat? There's nothing like a brisk walk to induce sound, restful sleep," he told them. He hummed a bar.

"You'll be all right, mother?" Lulu asked.

Mrs. Bett did not look up. "These cardamom hev got a little mite too dry," she said.

In their room, Ina and Dwight discussed the incredible actions of Lulu.

"I saw," said Dwight, "I saw she wasn't herself. I'd do anything to avoid having a scene—you know that." His glance swept a little anxiously his Ina. "You know that, don't you?" he sharply inquired.

"But I really think you ought to have written to Ninian about it," she now dared to say. "It's—it's not a nice position for Lulu."

"Nice? Well, but whom has she got to blame for it?"

"Why, Ninian," said Ina.

Dwight threw out his hands. "Herself," he said. "To tell you the truth, I was perfectly amazed at the way she snapped him up there in that restaurant."

"Why, but, Dwight—"

"Brazen," he said. "Oh, it was brazen."

"It was just fun, in the first place."

"But no really nice woman—" he shook his head.

"Dwight! Lulu *is* nice. The idea!"

He regarded her. "Would you have done that?" he would know.

Under his fond look, she softened, took his homage, accepted everything, was silent.

"Certainly not," he said. "Lulu's tastes are not fine like yours. I should never think of you as sisters."

"She's awfully good," Ina said feebly. Fifteen years of married life behind her—but this was sweet and she could not resist.

"She has excellent qualities." He admitted it. "But look at the position she's in—married to a man who tells her he has another wife in order to get free. Now, no really nice woman—"

"No really nice man—" Ina did say that much.

"Ah," said Dwight, "but *you* could never be in such a position. No, no. Lulu is sadly lacking somewhere."

Ina sighed, threw back her head, caught her lower lip with her upper, as might be in a hem. "What if it was Di?" she supposed.

"Di!" Dwight's look rebuked his wife. "Di," he said, "was born with ladylike feelings."

It was not yet ten o'clock. Bobby Larkin was permitted to stay until ten. From the veranda came the indistinguishable murmur of those young voices.

"Bobby," Di was saying within that murmur, "Bobby, you don't kiss me as if you really wanted to kiss me, to-night."

VI

September

The office of Dwight Herbert Deacon, Dentist, Gold Work a Speciality (sic) in black lettering, and Justice of the Peace in gold, was above a store which had been occupied by one unlucky tenant after another, and had suffered long periods of vacancy when ladies' aid societies served lunches there, under great white signs, badly lettered. Some months of disuse were now broken by the news that the store had been let to a music man. A music man, what on earth was that, Warbleton inquired.

The music man arrived, installed three pianos, and filled his window with sheet music, as sung by many ladies who swung in hammocks or kissed their hands on the music covers. While he was still moving in, Dwight Herbert Deacon wandered downstairs and stood informally in the door of the new store. The music man, a pleasant-faced chap of thirty-odd, was rubbing at the face of a piano.

"Hello, there!" he said. "Can I sell you an upright?"

"If I can take it out in pulling your teeth, you can," Dwight replied. "Or," said he, "I might marry you free, either one."

On this their friendship began. Thenceforth, when business was dull, the idle hours of both men were beguiled with idle gossip.

"How the dickens did you think of pianos for a line?" Dwight asked him once. "Now, my father was a dentist, so I came by it natural—never entered my head to be anything else. But *pianos*—"

The music man—his name was Neil Cornish—threw up his chin in a boyish fashion, and said he'd be jiggered if he knew. All up and down the Warbleton main street, the chances are that the answer would sound the same. "I'm studying law when I get the chance," said Cornish, as one who makes a bid to be thought of more highly.

"I see," said Dwight, respectfully dwelling on the verb.

Later on Cornish confided more to Dwight: He was to come by a little inheritance some day—not much, but something. Yes, it made a man feel a certain confidence. . . .

"*Don't* it?" said Dwight heartily, as if he knew.

Every one liked Cornish. He told funny stories, and he never compared Warbleton save to its advantage. So at last Dwight said tentatively at lunch:

"What if I brought that Neil Cornish up for supper, one of these nights?"

"Oh, Dwightie, do," said Ina. "If there's a man in town, let's know it."

"What if I brought him up to-night?"

Up went Ina's eyebrows. *To-night?*

"'Scalloped potatoes and meat loaf and sauce and bread and butter," Lulu contributed.

Cornish came to supper. He was what is known in Warbleton as dapper. This Ina saw as she emerged on the veranda in response to Dwight's informal halloo on his way upstairs. She herself was in white muslin, now much too snug, and a blue ribbon. To her greeting their guest replied in that engaging shyness which is not awkwardness. He moved in some pleasant web of gentleness and friendliness.

They asked him the usual questions, and he replied, rocking all the time with a faint undulating motion of head and shoulders: Warbleton was one of the prettiest little towns that he had ever seen. He liked the people—they seemed different. He was sure to like the place, already liked it. Lulu came to the door in Ninian's thin black-and-white gown. She shook hands with the stranger, not looking at him, and said, "Come to supper, all." Monona was already in her place, singing under-breath. Mrs. Bett, after hovering in the kitchen door, entered; but they forgot to introduce her.

"Where's Di?" asked Ina. "I declare that daughter of mine is never anywhere."

A brief silence ensued as they were seated. There being a guest, grace was to come, and Dwight said unintelligibly and like lightning a generic appeal to bless this food, forgive all our sins and finally save us. And there was something tremendous, in this ancient form whereby all stages of men bow in some now unrecognized recognition of the ceremonial of taking food to nourish life—and more.

At "Amen" Di flashed in, her offices at the mirror fresh upon her—perfect hair, silk dress turned up at the hem. She met Cornish, crimsoned, fluttered to her seat, joggled the table and, "Oh, dear," she said audibly to her mother, "I forgot my ring."

The talk was saved alive by a frank effort. Dwight served, making jests about everybody coming back for more. They went on with Warbleton happenings, improvements and openings; and the runaway. Cornish tried hard to make himself agreeable, not ingratiatingly but good-naturedly. He wished profoundly that before coming he had looked up some more stories in the back of the Musical Gazettes. Lulu surreptitiously pinched off an ant that was running at large upon the cloth and thereafter kept her eyes steadfastly on the sugar-bowl to see if it could be from *that.* Dwight pretended that those whom he was helping a second time were getting more than their share and facetiously landed on Di about eating so much that she would grow up and be married, first thing she knew. At the word "married" Di turned scarlet, laughed heartily and lifted her glass of water.

"And what instruments do you play?" Ina asked Cornish, in an unrelated effort to lift the talk to musical levels.

"Well, do you know," said the music man, "I can't play a thing. Don't know a black note from a white one."

"You don't? Why, Di plays very prettily," said Di's mother. "But then how can you tell what songs to order?" Ina cried.

"Oh, by the music houses. You go by the sales." For the first time it occurred to Cornish that this was ridiculous. "You know, I'm really studying law," he said, shyly and proudly. Law! How very interesting, from Ina. Oh, but won't he bring up some songs some evening, for them to try over? Her and Di? At this Di laughed and said that she was out of practice and lifted her glass of water. In the presence of adults Di made one weep, she was so slender, so young, so without defences, so intolerably sensitive to every contact, so in agony lest she be found wanting. It was amazing how unlike was this Di to the Di who had ensnared Bobby Larkin. What was one to think?

Cornish paid very little attention to her. To Lulu he said kindly, "Don't you play, Miss—?" He had not caught her name—no stranger ever did catch it. But Dwight now supplied it: "Miss

Lulu Bett," he explained with loud emphasis, and Lulu burned her slow red. This question Lulu had usually answered by telling how a felon had interrupted her lessons and she had stopped "taking"—a participle sacred to music, in Warbleton. This vignette had been a kind of epitome of Lulu's biography. But now Lulu was heard to say serenely:

"No, but I'm quite fond of it. I went to a lovely concert—two weeks ago."

They all listened. Strange indeed to think of Lulu as having had experiences of which they did not know.

"Yes," she said. "It was in Savannah, Georgia." She flushed, and lifted her eyes in a manner of faint defiance. "Of course," she said, "I don't know the names of all the different instruments they played, but there were a good many." She laughed pleasantly as a part of her sentence. "They had some lovely tunes," she said. She knew that the subject was not exhausted and she hurried on. "The hall was real large," she superadded, "and there were quite a good many people there. And it was too warm."

"I see," said Cornish, and said what he had been waiting to say: That he too had been in Savannah, Georgia.

Lulu lit with pleasure. "Well!" she said. And her mind worked and she caught at the moment before it had escaped. "Isn't it a pretty city?" she asked. And Cornish assented with the intense heartiness of the provincial. He, too, it seemed, had a conversational appearance to maintain by its own effort. He said that he had enjoyed being in that town and that he was there for two hours.

"I was there for a week." Lulu's superiority was really pretty.

"Have good weather?" Cornish selected next.

Oh, yes. And they saw all the different buildings—but at her "we" she flushed and was silenced. She was colouring and breathing quickly. This was the first bit of conversation of this sort of Lulu's life.

After supper Ina inevitably proposed croquet, Dwight pretended to try to escape and, with his irrepressible mien, talked about Ina, elaborate in his insistence on the third person—"She loves it, we have to humour her, you know how it is. Or no! You don't know! But you will"—and more of the same sort, everybody laughing heartily, save Lulu, who looked uncomfortable and wished that Dwight wouldn't, and Mrs. Bett, who paid no attention to anybody that night, not because she had not been introduced, an omission which she had not even noticed, but merely as another form of "tantrim." A self-indulgence.

They emerged for croquet. And there on the porch sat Jenny Plow and Bobby, waiting for Di to keep an old engagement, which Di pretended to have forgotten, and to be frightfully annoyed to have to keep. She met the objections of her parents with all the batteries of her coquetry, set for both Bobby and Cornish and, bold in the presence of "company," at last went laughing away. And in the minute areas of her consciousness she said to herself that Bobby would be more in love with her than ever because she had risked all to go with him; and that Cornish ought to be distinctly attracted to her because she had not stayed. She was as primitive as pollen.

Ina was vexed. She said so, pouting in a fashion which she should have outgrown with white muslin and blue ribbons, and she had outgrown none of these things.

"That just spoils croquet," she said. "I'm vexed. Now we can't have a real game."

From the side-door, where she must have been lingering among the waterproofs, Lulu stepped forth.

"I'll play a game," she said.

❧

When Cornish actually proposed to bring some music to the Deacons', Ina turned toward Dwight Herbert all the facets of her responsibility. And Ina's sense of responsibility toward Di was enormous, oppressive, primitive, amounting, in fact, toward this daughter of Dwight Herbert's late wife, to an ability to compress the offices of stepmotherhood into the functions of the lecture platform. Ina was a fountain of admonition. Her idea of a daughter, step or not, was that of a manufactured product, strictly, which you constantly pinched and moulded. She thought that a moral preceptor had the right to secrete precepts. Di got them all. But of course the crest of Ina's responsibility was to marry Di. This verb should be transitive only when lovers are speaking of each other, or the minister or magistrate is speaking of lovers. It should never be transitive when predicated of parents or any other third party. But it is. Ina was quite agitated by its transitiveness as she took to her husband her incredible responsibility.

"You know, Herbert," said Ina, "if this Mr. Cornish comes here *very* much, what we may expect."

"What may we expect?" demanded Dwight Herbert, crisply.

Ina always played his games, answered what he expected her to answer, pretended to be intuitive when she was not so, said "I know" when she didn't know at all. Dwight Herbert, on the other hand, did not even play her games when he knew perfectly what she meant, but pretended not to understand, made her repeat, made her explain. It was as if Ina *had* to please him for, say, a living; but as for that dentist, he had to please nobody. In the conversations of Dwight and Ina you saw the historical home forming in clots in the fluid wash of the community.

"He'll fall in love with Di," said Ina.

"And what of that? Little daughter will have many a man fall in love with her, *I* should say."

"Yes, but, Dwight, what do you think of him?"

"What do I think of him? My dear Ina, I have other things to think of."

"But we don't know anything about him, Dwight—a stranger so."

"On the other hand," said Dwight with dignity, "I know a good deal about him."

With a great air of having done the fatherly and found out about this stranger before bringing him into the home, Dwight now related a number of stray circumstances dropped by Cornish in their chance talks.

"He has a little inheritance coming to him—shortly," Dwight wound up.

"An inheritance—really? How much, Dwight?"

"Now isn't that like a woman. Isn't it?"

"I *thought* he was from a good family," said Ina.

"My mercenary little pussy!"

"Well," she said with a sigh, "I shouldn't be surprised if Di did really accept him. A young girl is awfully flattered when a good-looking older man pays her attention. Haven't you noticed that?"

Dwight informed her, with an air of immense abstraction, that he left all such matters to her. Being married to Dwight was like a perpetual rehearsal, with Dwight's self-importance for audience.

A few evenings later, Cornish brought up the music. There was something overpowering in this brown-haired chap against the background of his negligible little shop, his whole capital in his few pianos. For he looked hopefully ahead, woke with plans, regarded the children in the street as if, conceivably, children might come within the confines of his life as he imagined it. A preposterous little man. And a preposterous store, empty, echoing, bare of wall, the three pianos near the front, the remainder of the floor stretching away like the corridors of the lost. He was going to get a dark curtain, he explained, and furnish the back part of the store as his own room. What dignity in phrasing, but how mean that little room would look—cot bed, washbowl and pitcher, and little mirror—almost certainly a mirror with a wavy surface, almost certainly that.

"And then, you know," he always added, "I'm reading law."

The Plows had been asked in that evening. Bobby was there. They were, Dwight Herbert said, going to have a sing.

Di was to play. And Di was now embarked on the most difficult feat of her emotional life, the feat of remaining to Bobby Larkin the lure, the beloved lure, the while to Cornish she instinctively played the rôle of womanly little girl.

"Up by the festive lamp, everybody!" Dwight Herbert cried.

As they gathered about the upright piano, that startled, Dwightish instrument, standing in its attitude of unrest, Lulu came in with another lamp.

"Do you need this?" she asked.

They did not need it, there was, in fact, no place to set it, and this Lulu must have known. But Dwight found a place. He swept Ninian's photograph from the marble shelf of the mirror, and when Lulu had placed the lamp there, Dwight thrust the photograph into her hands.

"You take care of that," he said, with a droop of lid discernible only to those who—presumably—loved him. His old attitude toward Lulu had shown a terrible sharpening in these ten days since her return.

She stood uncertainly, in the thin black-and-white gown which Ninian had bought for her, and held Ninian's photograph and looked helplessly about. She was moving toward the door when Cornish called:

"See here! Aren't *you* going to sing?"

"What?" Dwight used the falsetto. "Lulu sing? *Lulu?*"

She stood awkwardly. She had a piteous recrudescence of her old agony at being spoken to in the presence of others. But Di had opened the *Album of Old Favourites*, which Cornish had elected to bring, and now she struck the opening chords of "Bonny Eloise." Lulu stood still, looking rather piteously at Cornish. Dwight offered his arm, absurdly crooked. The Plows and Ina and Di began to sing. Lulu moved forward, and stood a little away from them, and sang, too. She was still holding Ninian's picture. Dwight did not sing. He lifted his shoulders and his eyebrows and watched Lulu.

When they had finished, "Lulu the mocking bird!" Dwight cried. He said "ba-ird."

"Fine!" cried Cornish. "Why, Miss Lulu, you have a good voice!"

"Miss Lulu Bett, the mocking ba-ird!" Dwight insisted.

Lulu was excited, and in some accession of faint power. She turned to him now, quietly, and with a look of appraisal.

"Lulu the dove," she then surprisingly said, "to put up with you."

It was her first bit of conscious repartee to her brother-in-law.

Cornish was bending over Di.

"What next do you say?" he asked.

She lifted her eyes, met his own, held them. "There's such a lovely, lovely sacred song here," she suggested, and looked down.

"You like sacred music?"

She turned to him her pure profile, her eyelids fluttering up, and said: "I love it."

"That's it. So do I. Nothing like a nice sacred piece," Cornish declared.

Bobby Larkin, at the end of the piano, looked directly into Di's face.

"Give *me* ragtime," he said now, with the effect of bursting out of somewhere. "Don't you like ragtime?" he put it to her directly.

Di's eyes danced into his, they sparkled for him, her smile was a smile for him alone, all their store of common memories was in their look.

"Let's try 'My Rock, My Refuge,'" Cornish suggested. "That's got up real attractive."

Di's profile again, and her pleased voice saying that this was the very one she had been hoping to hear him sing.

They gathered for "My Rock, My Refuge."

"Oh," cried Ina, at the conclusion of this number, "I'm having such a perfectly beautiful time. Isn't everybody?" everybody's hostess put it.

"Lulu is," said Dwight, and added softly to Lulu: "She don't have to hear herself sing."

It was incredible. He was like a bad boy with a frog. About that photograph of Ninian he found a dozen ways to torture her, called attention to it, showed it to Cornish, set it on the piano facing them all. Everybody must have understood—excepting the Plows. These two gentle souls sang placidly through the *Album of Old Favourites*, and at the melodies smiled happily upon each other with an air from another world. Always it was as if the Plows walked some fair, inter-penetrating plane, from which they looked out as do other things not quite of earth, say, flowers and fire and music.

Strolling home that night, the Plows were overtaken by some one who ran badly, and as if she were unaccustomed to running.

"Mis' Plow, Mis' Plow!" this one called, and Lulu stood beside them.

"Say!" she said. "Do you know of any job that I could get me? I mean that I'd know how to do? A job for money . . . I mean a job . . ."

She burst into passionate crying. They drew her home with them.

Lying awake sometime after midnight, Lulu heard the telephone ring. She heard Dwight's concerned "Is that so?" And his cheerful "Be right there."

Grandma Gates was sick, she heard him tell Ina. In a few moments he ran down the stairs. Next day they told how Dwight had sat for hours that night, holding Grandma Gates so that her back would rest easily and she could fight for her faint breath. The kind fellow had only about two hours of sleep the whole night long.

Next day there came a message from that woman who had brought up Dwight—"made him what he was," he often complacently accused her. It was a note on a postal card—she had often written a few lines on a postal card to say that she had sent the maple sugar, or could Ina get her some samples. Now she wrote a few lines on a postal card to say that she was going to die with cancer. Could Dwight and Ina come to her while she was still able to visit? If he was not too busy . . .

Nobody saw the pity and the terror of that postal card. They stuck it up by the kitchen clock to read over from time to time, and before they left, Dwight lifted the griddle of the cooking-stove and burned the postal card.

And before they left Lulu said: "Dwight—you can't tell how long you'll be gone?"

"Of course not. How should I tell?"

"No. And that letter might come while you're away."

"Conceivably. Letters do come while a man's away!"

"Dwight—I thought if you wouldn't mind if I opened it—"

"Opened it?"

"Yes. You see, it'll be about me mostly—"

"I should have said that it'll be about my brother mostly."

"But you know what I mean. You wouldn't mind if I did open it?"

"But you say you know what'll be in it."

"So I did know—till you—I've got to see that letter, Dwight."

"And so you shall. But not till I show it to you. My dear Lulu, you know how I hate having my mail interfered with."

She might have said: "Small souls always make a point of that." She said nothing. She watched them set off, and kept her mind on Ina's thousand injunctions.

"Don't let Di see much of Bobby Larkin. And, Lulu—if it occurs to her to have Mr. Cornish come up to sing, of course you ask him. You might ask him to supper. And don't let mother overdo. And, Lulu, now do watch Monona's handkerchief—the child will never take a clean one if I'm not here to tell her. . . ."

She breathed injunctions to the very step of the bus.

In the bus Dwight leaned forward:

"See that you play post-office squarely, Lulu!" he called, and threw back his head and lifted his eyebrows.

In the train he turned tragic eyes to his wife.

"Ina," he said. "It's *ma.* And she's going to die. It can't be. . . ."

Ina said: "But you're going to help her, Dwight, just being there with her."

It was true that the mere presence of the man would bring a kind of fresh life to that worn frame. Tact and wisdom and love would speak through him and minister.

Toward the end of their week's absence the letter from Ninian came.

Lulu took it from the post-office when she went for the mail that evening, dressed in her dark red gown. There was no other letter, and she carried that one letter in her hand all through the streets. She passed those who were surmising what her story might be, who were telling one another what they had heard. But she knew hardly more than they. She passed Cornish in the doorway of his little music shop, and spoke with him; and there was the letter. It was so that Dwight's foster mother's postal card might have looked on its way to be mailed.

Cornish stepped down and overtook her.

"Oh, Miss Lulu. I've got a new song or two—"

She said abstractedly: "Do. Any night. To-morrow night—could you—" It was as if Lulu were too preoccupied to remember to be ill at ease.

Cornish flushed with pleasure, said that he could indeed.

"Come for supper," Lulu said.

Oh, could he? Wouldn't that be . . . Well, say! Such was his acceptance.

He came for supper. And Di was not at home. She had gone off in the country with Jenny and Bobby, and they merely did not return.

Mrs. Bett and Lulu and Cornish and Monona supped alone. All were at ease, now that they were alone. Especially Mrs. Bett was at ease. It became one of her young nights, her alive and lucid nights. She was *there*. She sat in Dwight's chair and Lulu sat in Ina's chair. Lulu had picked flowers for the table—a task coveted by her but usually performed by Ina. Lulu had now picked Sweet William and had filled a vase of silver gilt taken from the parlour. Also, Lulu had made ice-cream.

"I don't see what Di can be thinking of," Lulu said. "It seems like asking you under false—" She was afraid of "pretences" and ended without it.

Cornish savoured his steaming beef pie, with sage. "Oh, well!" he said contentedly.

"Kind of a relief, *I* think, to have her gone," said Mrs. Bett, from the fulness of something or other.

"Mother!" Lulu said, twisting her smile.

"Why, my land, I love her," Mrs. Bett explained, "but she wiggles and chitters."

Cornish never made the slightest effort, at any time, to keep a straight face. The honest fellow now laughed loudly.

"Well!" Lulu thought. "He can't be so *very* much in love." And again she thought: "He doesn't know anything about the letter. He thinks Ninian got tired of me." Deep in her heart there abode her certainty that this was not so.

By some etiquette of consent, Mrs. Bett cleared the table and Lulu and Cornish went into the parlour. There lay the letter on the drop-leaf side-table, among the shells. Lulu had carried it there, where she need not see it at her work. The letter looked no more than the advertisement of dental office furniture beneath it. Monona stood indifferently fingering both.

"Monona," Lulu said sharply, "leave them be!"

Cornish was displaying his music. "Got up quite attractive," he said—it was his formula of praise for his music.

"But we can't try it over," Lulu said, "if Di doesn't come."

"Well, say," said Cornish shyly, "you know I left that *Album of Old Favourites* here. Some of them we know by heart."

Lulu looked. "I'll tell you something," she said, "there's some of these I can play with one hand—by ear. Maybe—"

"Why sure!" said Cornish.

Lulu sat at the piano. She had on the wool chally, long sacred to the nights when she must combine her servant's estate with the quality of being Ina's sister. She wore her coral beads and her cameo cross. In her absence she had caught the trick of dressing her hair so that it looked even more abundant—but she had not dared to try it so until to-night, when Dwight was gone. Her long wrist was curved high, her thin hand pressed and fingered awkwardly, and at her mistakes her head dipped and strove to make all right. Her foot continuously touched the loud pedal—the blurred sound seemed to accomplish more. So she played "How Can I Leave Thee," and they managed to sing it. So she played "Long, Long Ago," and "Little Nell of Narragansett Bay." Beyond open doors, Mrs. Bett listened, sang, it may be, with them; for when the singers ceased, her voice might be heard still humming a loud closing bar.

"Well!" Cornish cried to Lulu; and then, in the formal village phrase: "You're quite a musician."

"Oh, no!" Lulu disclaimed it. She looked up, flushed, smiling. "I've never done this in front of anybody," she owned. "I don't know what Dwight and Ina'd say. . . ." She drooped.

They rested, and, miraculously, the air of the place had stirred and quickened, as if the crippled, halting melody had some power of its own, and poured this forth, even thus trampled.

"I guess you could do 'most anything you set your hand to," said Cornish.

"Oh, no," Lulu said again.

"Sing and play and cook—"

"But I can't earn anything. I'd like to earn something." But this she had not meant to say. She stopped, rather frightened.

"You would! Why, you have it fine here, I thought."

"Oh, fine, yes. Dwight gives me what I have. And I do their work."

"I see," said Cornish. "I never thought of that," he added. She caught his speculative look—he had heard a tale or two concerning her return, as who in Warbleton had not heard?

"You're wondering why I didn't stay with him!" Lulu said recklessly. This was no less than wrung from her, but its utterance occasioned in her an unspeakable relief.

"Oh, no," Cornish disclaimed, and coloured and rocked.

"Yes, you are," she swept on. "The whole town's wondering. Well, I'd like 'em to know, but Dwight won't let me tell."

Cornish frowned, trying to understand.

"'Won't let you!'" he repeated. "I should say that was your own affair."

"No. Not when Dwight gives me all I have."

"Oh, that—" said Cornish. "That's not right."

"No. But there it is. It puts me—you see what it does to me. They think—they all think my—husband left me."

It was curious to hear her bring out that word—tentatively, deprecatingly, like some one daring a foreign phrase without warrant.

Cornish said feebly: "Oh, well . . ."

Before she willed it, she was telling him:

"He didn't. He didn't leave me," she cried with passion. "He had another wife." Incredibly it was as if she were defending both him and herself.

"Lord sakes!" said Cornish.

She poured it out, in her passion to tell some one, to share her news of her state where there would be neither hardness nor censure.

"We were in Savannah, Georgia," she said. "We were going to leave for Oregon—going to go through California. We were in the hotel, and he was going out to get the tickets. He started to go. Then he came back. I was sitting the same as there. He opened the door again—the same as here. I saw he looked different—and he said quick: 'There's something you'd ought to know before we go.' And of course I said, 'What?' And he said it right out—how he was married eighteen years ago and in two years she ran away and she must be dead but he wasn't sure. He hadn't the proofs. So of course I came home. But it wasn't him left me."

"No, no. Of course he didn't," Cornish said earnestly. "But Lord sakes—" he said again. He rose to walk about, found it impracticable and sat down.

"That's what Dwight don't want me to tell—he thinks it isn't true. He thinks—he didn't have any other wife. He thinks he wanted—" Lulu looked up at him. "You see," she said, "Dwight thinks he didn't want me."

"But why don't you make your—husband—I mean, why doesn't he write to Mr. Deacon here, and tell him the truth—" Cornish burst out.

Under this implied belief, she relaxed and into her face came its rare sweetness.

"He has written," she said. "The letter's there."

He followed her look, scowled at the two letters.

"What'd he say?"

"Dwight don't like me to touch his mail. I'll have to wait till he comes back."

"Lord sakes!" said Cornish.

This time he did rise and walk about. He wanted to say something, wanted it with passion. He paused beside Lulu and stammered:

"You—you—you're too nice a girl to get a deal like this. Darned if you aren't."

To her own complete surprise Lulu's eyes filled with tears, and she could not speak. She was by no means above self-sympathy.

"And there ain't," said Cornish sorrowfully, "there ain't a thing I can do."

And yet he was doing much. He was gentle, he was listening, and on his face a frown of concern. His face continually surprised her, it was so fine and alive and near, by comparison with Ninian's loose-lipped, ruddy, impersonal look and Dwight's thin, high-boned hardness. All the time Cornish gave her something, instead of drawing upon her. Above all, he was there, and she could talk to him.

"It's—it's funny," Lulu said. "I'd be awful glad if I just *could* know for sure that the other woman was alive—if I couldn't know she's dead."

This surprising admission Cornish seemed to understand.

"Sure you would," he said briefly.

"Cora Waters," Lulu said. "Cora Waters, of San Diego, California. And she never heard of me."

"No," Cornish admitted. They stared at each other as across some abyss.

In the doorway Mrs. Bett appeared.

"I scraped up everything," she remarked, "and left the dishes set."

"That's right, mamma," Lulu said. "Come and sit down."

Mrs. Bett entered with a leisurely air of doing the thing next expected of her.

"I don't hear any more playin' and singin'," she remarked. "It sounded real nice."

"We—we sung all I knew how to play, I guess, mamma."

"I use' to play on the melodeon," Mrs. Bett volunteered, and spread and examined her right hand.

"Well!" said Cornish.

She now told them about her log-house in a New England clearing, when she was a bride. All her store of drama and life came from her. She rehearsed it with far eyes. She laughed at old delights, drooped at old fears. She told about her little daughter who had died at sixteen—a tragedy such as once would have been renewed in a vital ballad. At the end she yawned frankly as if, in some terrible sophistication, she had been telling the story of some one else.

"Give us one more piece," she said.

"Can we?" Cornish asked.

"I can play 'I Think When I Read That Sweet Story of Old,'" Lulu said.

"That's the ticket!" cried Cornish.

They sang it, to Lulu's right hand.

"That's the one you picked out when you was a little girl, Lulie," cried Mrs. Bett.

Lulu had played it now as she must have played it then.

Half after nine and Di had not returned. But nobody thought of Di. Cornish rose to go.

"What's them?" Mrs. Bett demanded.

"Dwight's letters, mamma. You mustn't touch them!" Lulu's voice was sharp.

"Say!" Cornish, at the door, dropped his voice. "If there was anything I could do at any time, you'd let me know, wouldn't you?"

That past tense, those subjunctives, unconsciously called upon her to feel no intrusion.

"Oh, thank you," she said. "You don't know how good it is to feel—"

"Of course it is," said Cornish heartily.

They stood for a moment on the porch. The night was one of low clamour from the grass, tiny voices, insisting.

"Of course," said Lulu, "of course you won't—you wouldn't—"

"Say anything?" he divined. "Not for dollars. Not," he repeated, "for dollars."

"But I knew you wouldn't," she told him.

He took her hand. "Good-night," he said. "I've had an awful nice time singing and listening to you talk—well, of course—I mean," he cried, "the supper was just fine. And so was the music."

"Oh, no," she said.

Mrs. Bett came into the hall.

"Lulie," she said, "I guess you didn't notice—this one's from Ninian."

"Mother—"

"I opened it—why, of course I did. It's from Ninian."

Mrs. Bett held out the opened envelope, the unfolded letter, and a yellowed newspaper clipping.

"See," said the old woman, "says, 'Corie Waters, music hall singer—married last night to Ninian Deacon—' Say, Lulie, that must be her. . . ."

Lulu threw out her hands.

"There!" she cried triumphantly. "He *was* married to her, just like he said!"

❧

❧

The Plows were at breakfast next morning when Lulu came in casually at the side-door. Yes, she said, she had had breakfast. She merely wanted to see them about something. Then she said nothing, but sat looking with a troubled frown at Jenny. Jenny's hair was about her neck, like the hair of a little girl, a south window poured light upon her, the fruit and honey upon the table seemed her only possible food.

"You look troubled, Lulu," Mrs. Plow said. "Is it about getting work?"

"No," said Lulu, "no. I've been places to ask—quite a lot of places. I guess the bakery is going to let me make cake."

"I knew it would come to you," Mrs. Plow said, and Lulu thought that this was a strange way to speak, when she herself had gone after the cakes. But she kept on looking about the room. It was so bright and quiet. As she came in, Mr. Plow had been reading from a book. Dwight never read from a book at table.

"I wish—" said Lulu, as she looked at them. But she did not know what she wished. Certainly it was for no moral excellence, for she perceived none.

"What is it, Lulu?" Mr. Plow asked, and he was bright and quiet too, Lulu thought.

"Well," said Lulu, "it's not much. But I wanted Jenny to tell me about last night."

"Last night?"

"Yes. Would you—" Hesitation was her only way of apology. "Where did you go?" She turned to Jenny.

Jenny looked up in her clear and ardent fashion: "We went across the river and carried supper and then we came home."

"What time did you get home?"

"Oh, it was still light. Long before eight, it was."

Lulu hesitated and flushed, asked how long Di and Bobby had stayed there at Jenny's; whereupon she heard that Di had to be home early on account of Mr. Cornish, so that she and Bobby had not stayed at all. To which Lulu said an "of course," but first she stared at Jenny and so impaired the strength of her assent. Almost at once she rose to go.

"Nothing else?" said Mrs. Plow, catching that look of hers.

Lulu wanted to say: "My husband *was* married before, just as he said he was." But she said nothing more, and went home. There she put it to Di, and with her terrible bluntness reviewed to Di the testimony.

"You were not with Jenny after eight o'clock. Where were you?" Lulu spoke formally and her rehearsals were evident.

Di said: "When mamma comes home, I'll tell her."

With this Lulu had no idea how to deal, and merely looked at her helplessly. Mrs. Bett, who was lacing her shoes, now said casually:

"No need to wait till then. Her and Bobby were out in the side yard sitting in the hammock till all hours."

Di had no answer save her furious flush, and Mrs. Bett went on:

"Didn't I tell you? I knew it before the company left, but I didn't say a word. Thinks I, 'She's wiggles and chitters.' So I left her stay where she was."

"But, mother!" Lulu cried. "You didn't even tell me after he'd gone."

"I forgot it," Mrs. Bett said, "finding Ninian's letter and all—" She talked of Ninian's letter.

Di was bright and alert and firm of flesh and erect before Lulu's softness and laxness.

"I don't know what your mother'll say," said Lulu, "and I don't know what people'll think."

"They won't think Bobby and I are tired of each other, anyway," said Di, and left the room.

Through the day Lulu tried to think what she must do. About Di she was anxious and felt without power. She thought of the indignation of Dwight and Ina that Di had not been more scrupulously guarded. She thought of Di's girlish folly, her irritating independence—"and there," Lulu thought, "just the other day I was teaching her to sew." Her mind dwelt too on Dwight's furious anger at the opening of Ninian's letter. But when all this had spent itself, what was she herself to do? She must leave his house before he ordered her to do so, when she told him that she had confided in Cornish, as tell she must. But what was she to *do*? The bakery cake-making would not give her a roof.

Stepping about the kitchen in her blue cotton gown, her hair tight and flat as seemed proper when one was not dressed, she thought about these things. And it was strange: Lulu bore no physical appearance of one in distress or any anxiety. Her head was erect, her movements were strong and swift, her eyes were interested. She was no drooping Lulu with dragging step. She was more intent, she was somehow more operative than she had ever been.

Mrs. Bett was working contentedly beside her, and now and then humming an air of that music of the night before. The sun surged through the kitchen door and east window, a returned oriole swung and fluted on the elm above the gable. Wagons clattered by over the rattling wooden block pavement.

"Ain't it nice with nobody home?" Mrs. Bett remarked at intervals, like the burden of a comic song.

"Hush, mother," Lulu said, troubled, her ethical refinements conflicting with her honesty.

"Speak the truth and shame the devil," Mrs. Bett contended.

When dinner was ready at noon, Di did not appear. A little earlier Lulu had heard her moving about her room, and she served her in expectation that she would join them.

"Di must be having the 'tantrim' this time," she thought, and for a time said nothing. But at length she did say: "Why doesn't Di come? I'd better put her plate in the oven."

Rising to do so, she was arrested by her mother. Mrs. Bett was eating a baked potato, holding her fork close to the tines, and presenting a profile of passionate absorption.

"Why, Di went off," she said.

"Went off!"

"Down the walk. Down the sidewalk."

"She must have gone to Jenny's," said Lulu. "I wish she wouldn't do that without telling me."

Monona laughed out and shook her straight hair. "She'll catch it!" she cried in sisterly enjoyment.

It was when Lulu had come back from the kitchen and was seated at the table that Mrs. Bett observed:

"I didn't think Inie'd want her to take her nice new satchel."

"Her satchel?"

"Yes. Inie wouldn't take it north herself, but Di had it."

"Mother," said Lulu, "when Di went away just now, was she carrying a satchel?"

"Didn't I just tell you?" Mrs. Bett demanded, aggrieved. "I said I didn't think Inie—"

"Mother! Which way did she go?"

Monona pointed with her spoon. "She went that way," she said. "I seen her."

Lulu looked at the clock. For Monona had pointed toward the railway station. The twelve-thirty train, which every one took to the city for shopping, would be just about leaving.

"Monona," said Lulu, "don't you go out of the yard while I'm gone. Mother, you keep her—"

Lulu ran from the house and up the street. She was in her blue cotton dress, her old shoes, she was hatless and without money. When she was still two or three blocks from the station, she heard the twelve-thirty "pulling out."

She ran badly, her ankles in their low, loose shoes continually turning, her arms held taut at her sides. So she came down the platform, and to the ticket window. The contained ticket man, wonted to lost trains and perturbed faces, yet actually ceased counting when he saw her:

"Lenny! Did Di Deacon take that train?"

"Sure she did," said Lenny.

"And Bobby Larkin?" Lulu cared nothing for appearances now.

"He went in on the Local," said Lenny, and his eyes widened.

"Where?"

"See." Lenny thought it through. "Millton," he said. "Yes, sure. Millton. Both of 'em."

"How long till another train?"

"Well, sir," said the ticket man, "you're in luck, if you was goin' too. Seventeen was late this morning—she'll be along, jerk of a lamb's tail."

"Then," said Lulu, "you got to give me a ticket to Millton, without me paying till after—and you got to lend me two dollars."

"Sure thing," said Lenny, with a manner of laying the entire railway system at her feet.

"Seventeen" would rather not have stopped at Warbleton, but Lenny's signal was law on the time card, and the magnificent yellow express slowed down for Lulu. Hatless and in her blue cotton gown, she climbed aboard.

Then her old inefficiency seized upon her. What was she going to do? Millton! She had been there but once, years ago—how could she ever find anybody? Why had she not stayed in Warbleton and asked the sheriff or somebody—no, not the sheriff. Cornish, perhaps. Oh, and Dwight and Ina were going to be angry now! And Di—little Di. As Lulu thought of her she began to cry. She said to herself that she had taught Di to sew.

In sight of Millton, Lulu was seized with trembling and physical nausea. She had never been alone in any unfamiliar town. She put her hands to her hair and for the first time realized her rolled-up sleeves. She was pulling down these sleeves when the conductor came through the train.

"Could you tell me," she said timidly, "the name of the principal hotel in Millton?"

Ninian had asked this as they neared Savannah, Georgia.

The conductor looked curiously at her.

"Why, the Hess House," he said. "Wasn't you expecting anybody to meet you?" he asked, kindly.

"No," said Lulu, "but I'm going to find my folks—" Her voice trailed away.

"Beats all," thought the conductor, using his utility formula for the universe.

In Millton Lulu's inquiry for the Hess House produced no consternation. Nobody paid any attention to her. She was almost certainly taken to be a new servant there.

"You stop feeling so!" she said to herself angrily at the lobby entrance. "Ain't you been to that big hotel in Savannah, Georgia?"

The Hess House, Millton, had a tradition of its own to maintain, it seemed, and they sent her to the rear basement door. She obeyed meekly, but she lost a good deal of time before she found herself at the end of the office desk. It was still longer before any one attended her.

"Please, sir!" she burst out. "See if Di Deacon has put her name on your book."

Her appeal was tremendous, compelling. The young clerk listened to her, showed her where to look in the register. When only strange names and strange writing presented themselves there, he said:

"Tried the parlour?"

And directed her kindly and with his thumb, and in the other hand a pen divorced from his ear for the express purpose.

In crossing the lobby in the hotel at Savannah, Georgia, Lulu's most pressing problem had been to know where to look. But now the idlers in the Hess House lobby did not exist. In time she found the door of the intensely rose-coloured reception room. There, in a fat, rose-coloured chair, beside a cataract of lace curtain, sat Di, alone.

Lulu entered. She had no idea what to say. When Di looked up, started up, frowned, Lulu felt as if she herself were the culprit. She said the first thing that occurred to her:

"I don't believe mamma'll like your taking her nice satchel."

"Well!" said Di, exactly as if she had been at home. And superadded: "My goodness!" And then cried rudely: "What are you here for?"

"For you," said Lulu. "You—you—you'd ought not to be here, Di."

"What's that to you?" Di cried.

"Why, Di, you're just a little girl—" Lulu saw that this was all wrong, and stopped miserably. How was she to go on? "Di," she said, "if you and Bobby want to get married, why not let us get you up a nice wedding at home?" And she saw that this sounded as if she were talking about a tea party.

"Who said we wanted to be married?"

"Well, he's here."

"Who said he's here?"

"Isn't he?"

Di sprang up. "Aunt Lulu," she said, "you're a funny person to be telling *me* what to do."

Lulu said, flushing: "I love you just the same as if I was married happy, in a home."

"Well, you aren't!" cried Di cruelly, "and I'm going to do just as I think best."

Lulu thought this over, her look grave and sad. She tried to find something to say. "What do people say to people," she wondered, "when it's like this?"

"Getting married is for your whole life," was all that came to her.

"Yours wasn't," Di flashed at her.

Lulu's colour deepened, but there seemed to be no resentment in her. She must deal with this right—that was what her manner seemed to say. And how should she deal?

"Di," she cried, "come back with me—and wait till mamma and papa get home."

"That's likely. They say I'm not to be married till I'm twenty-one."

"Well, but how young that is!"

"It is to you."

"Di! This is wrong—it *is* wrong."

"There's nothing wrong about getting married—if you stay married."

"Well, then it can't be wrong to let them know."

"It isn't. But they'd treat me wrong. They'd make me stay at home. And I won't stay at home—I won't stay there. They act as if I was ten years old."

Abruptly in Lulu's face there came a light of understanding.

"Why, Di," she said, "do you feel that way too?"

Di missed this. She went on:

"I'm grown up. I feel just as grown up as they do. And I'm not allowed to do a thing I feel. I want to be away—I will be away!"

"I know about that part," Lulu said.

She now looked at Di with attention. Was it possible that Di was suffering in the air of that home as she herself suffered? She had not thought of that. There Di had seemed so young, so dependent, so—asquirm. Here, by herself, waiting for Bobby, in the Hess House at Millton, she was curiously adult. Would she be adult if she were let alone?

"You don't know what it's like," Di cried, "to be hushed up and laughed at and paid no attention to, everything you say."

"Don't I?" said Lulu. "Don't I?"

She was breathing quickly and looking at Di. If *this* was why Di was leaving home . . .

"But, Di," she cried, "do you love Bobby Larkin?"

By this Di was embarrassed. "I've got to marry somebody," she said, "and it might as well be him."

"But is it him?"

"Yes, it is," said Di. "But," she added, "I know I could love almost anybody real nice that was nice to me." And this she said, not in her own right, but either she had picked it up somewhere and adopted it, or else the terrible modernity and honesty of her day somehow spoke through her, for its own. But to Lulu it was as if something familiar turned its face to be recognised.

"Di!" she cried.

"It's true. You ought to know that." She waited for a moment. "You did it," she added. "Mamma said so."

At this onslaught Lulu was stupefied. For she began to perceive its truth.

"I know what I want to do, I guess," Di muttered, as if to try to cover what she had said.

Up to that moment, Lulu had been feeling intensely that she understood Di, but that Di did not know this. Now Lulu felt that she and Di actually shared some unsuspected sisterhood. It was not only that they were both badgered by Dwight. It was more than that. They were two women. And she must make Di know that she understood her.

"Di," Lulu said, breathing hard, "what you just said is true, I guess. Don't you think I don't know. And now I'm going to tell you—"

She might have poured it all out, claimed her kinship with Di by virtue of that which had happened in Savannah, Georgia. But Di said:

"Here come some ladies. And goodness, look at the way you look!"

Lulu glanced down. "I know," she said, "but I guess you'll have to put up with me."

The two women entered, looked about with the complaisance of those who examine a hotel property, find criticism incumbent, and have no errand. These two women had outdressed their occasion. In their presence Di kept silence, turned away her head, gave them to know that she had nothing to do with this blue cotton person beside her. When they had gone on, "What do you mean by my having to put up with you?" Di asked sharply.

"I mean I'm going to stay with you."

Di laughed scornfully—she was again the rebellious child. "I guess Bobby'll have something to say about that," she said insolently.

"They left you in my charge."

"But I'm not a baby—the idea, Aunt Lulu!"

"I'm going to stay right with you," said Lulu. She wondered what she should do if Di suddenly marched away from her, through that bright lobby and into the street. She thought miserably that she must follow. And then her whole concern for the ethics of Di's course was lost in her agonised memory of her terrible, broken shoes.

Di did not march away. She turned her back squarely upon Lulu, and looked out of the window. For her life Lulu could think of nothing more to say. She was now feeling miserably on the defensive.

They were sitting in silence when Bobby Larkin came into the room.

Four Bobby Larkins there were, in immediate succession.

The Bobby who had just come down the street was distinctly perturbed, came hurrying, now and then turned to the left when he met folk, glanced sidewise here and there, was altogether anxious and ill at ease.

The Bobby who came through the hotel was a Bobby who had on an importance assumed for the crisis of threading the lobby—a Bobby who wished it to be understood that here he was, a man among men, in the Hess House at Millton.

The Bobby who entered the little rose room was the Bobby who was no less than overwhelmed with the stupendous character of the adventure upon which he found himself.

The Bobby who incredibly came face to face with Lulu was the real Bobby into whose eyes leaped instant, unmistakable relief.

Di flew to meet him. She assumed all the pretty agitations of her rôle, ignored Lulu.

"Bobby! Is it all right?"

Bobby looked over her head.

"Miss Lulu," he said fatuously. "If it ain't Miss Lulu."

He looked from her to Di, and did not take in Di's resigned shrug.

"Bobby," said Di, "she's come to stop us getting married, but she can't. I've told her so."

"She don't have to stop us," quoth Bobby gloomily, "we're stopped."

"What do you mean?" Di laid one hand flatly along her cheek, instinctive in her melodrama.

Bobby drew down his brows, set his hand on his leg, elbow out.

"We're minors," said he.

"Well, gracious, you didn't have to tell them that."

"No. They knew *I* was."

"But, silly! Why didn't you tell them you're not?"

"But I am."

Di stared. "For pity sakes," she said, "don't you know how to do anything?"

"What would you have me do?" he inquired indignantly, with his head held very stiff, and with a boyish, admirable lift of chin.

"Why, tell them we're both twenty-one. We look it. We know we're responsible—that's all they care for. Well, you are a funny . . ."

"You wanted me to lie?" he said.

"Oh, don't make out you never told a fib."

"Well, but this—" he stared at her.

"I never heard of such a thing," Di cried accusingly.

"Anyhow," he said, "there's nothing to do now. The cat's out. I've told our ages. We've got to have our folks in on it."

"Is that all you can think of?" she demanded.

"What else?"

"Why, come on to Bainbridge or Holt, and tell them we're of age, and be married there."

"Di," said Bobby, "why, that'd be a rotten go."

Di said, oh very well, if he didn't want to marry her. He replied stonily that of course he wanted to marry her. Di stuck out her little hand. She was at a disadvantage. She could use no arts, with Lulu sitting there, looking on. "Well, then, come on to Bainbridge," Di cried, and rose.

Lulu was thinking: "What shall I say? I don't know what to say. I don't know what I can say." Now she also rose, and laughed awkwardly. "I've told Di," she said to Bobby, "that wherever you two go, I'm going too. Di's folks left her in my care, you know. So you'll have to take me along, I guess." She spoke in a manner of distinct apology.

At this Bobby had no idea what to reply. He looked down miserably at the carpet. His whole manner was a mute testimony to his participation in the eternal query: How did I get into it?

"Bobby," said Di, "are you going to let her lead you home?"

This of course nettled him, but not in the manner on which Di had counted. He said loudly:

"I'm not going to Bainbridge or Holt or any town and lie, to get you or any other girl."

Di's head lifted, tossed, turned from him. "You're about as much like a man in a story," she said, "as—as papa is."

The two idly inspecting women again entered the rose room,

this time to stay. They inspected Lulu too. And Lulu rose and stood between the lovers.

"Hadn't we all better get the four-thirty to Warbleton?" she said, and swallowed.

"Oh, if Bobby wants to back out—" said Di.

"I don't want to back out," Bobby contended furiously, "b-b-but I won't—"

"Come on, Aunt Lulu," said Di grandly.

Bobby led the way through the lobby, Di followed, and Lulu brought up the rear. She walked awkwardly, eyes down, her hands stiffly held. Heads turned to look at her. They passed into the street.

"You two go ahead," said Lulu, "so they won't think—"

They did so, and she followed, and did not know where to look, and thought of her broken shoes.

At the station, Bobby put them on the train and stepped back. He had, he said, something to see to there in Millton. Di did not look at him. And Lulu's good-bye spoke her genuine regret for all.

"Aunt Lulu," said Di, "you needn't think I'm going to sit with you. You look as if you were crazy. I'll sit back here."

"All right, Di," said Lulu humbly.

It was nearly six o'clock when they arrived at the Deacons'. Mrs. Bett stood on the porch, her hands rolled in her apron.

"Surprise for you!" she called brightly.

Before they had reached the door, Ina bounded from the hall.

"Darling!"

She seized upon Di, kissed her loudly, drew back from her, saw the travelling bag.

"My new bag!" she cried. "Di! What have you got that for?"

In any embarrassment Di's instinctive defence was hearty laughter. She now laughed heartily, kissed her mother again, and ran up the stairs.

Lulu slipped by her sister, and into the kitchen.

"Well, where have *you* been?" cried Ina. "I declare, I never saw such a family. Mamma don't know anything and neither of you will tell anything."

"Mamma knows a-plenty," snapped Mrs. Bett.

Monona, who was eating a sticky gift, jumped stiffly up and down.

"You'll catch it—you'll catch it!" she sent out her shrill general warning.

Mrs. Bett followed Lulu to the kitchen: "I didn't tell Inie about her bag and now she says I don't know nothing," she complained. "There I knew about the bag the hull time, but I wasn't going to tell her and spoil her gettin' home." She banged the stove-griddle. "I've a good notion not to eat a mouthful o' supper," she announced.

"Mother, please!" said Lulu passionately. "Stay here. Help me. I've got enough to get through to-night."

Dwight had come home. Lulu could hear Ina pouring out to him the mysterious circumstance of the bag, could hear the exaggerated air of the casual with which he always received the excitement of another, and especially of his Ina. Then she heard Ina's feet padding up the stairs, and after that Di's shrill, nervous laughter. Lulu felt a pang of pity for Di, as if she herself were about to face them.

There was not time both to prepare supper and to change the blue cotton dress. In that dress Lulu was pouring water when Dwight entered the dining-room.

"Ah!" said he. "Our festive ball-gown."

She gave him her hand, with her peculiar sweetness of expression—almost as if she were sorry for him or were bidding him good-bye.

"*That* shows who you dress for!" he cried. "You dress for me. Ina, aren't you jealous? Lulu dresses for me!"

Ina had come in with Di, and both were excited, and Ina's head was moving stiffly, as in all her indignations. Mrs. Bett had thought better of it and had given her presence. Already Monona was singing.

"Lulu," said Dwight, "really? Can't you run up and slip on another dress?"

Lulu sat down in her place. "No," she said. "I'm too tired. I'm sorry, Dwight."

"It seems to me—" he began.

"I don't want any," said Monona.

But no one noticed Monona, and Ina did not defer even to Dwight. She, who measured delicate, troy occasions by avoirdupois, said brightly:

"Now, Di. You must tell us all about it. Where had you and Aunt Lulu been with mamma's new bag?"

"Aunt Lulu!" cried Dwight. "Aha! So Aunt Lulu was along. Well now, that alters it."

"How does it?" asked his Ina crossly.

"Why, when Aunt Lulu goes on a jaunt," said Dwight Herbert, "events begin to event."

"Come, Di, let's hear," said Ina.

"Ina," said Lulu, "first can't we hear something about your visit? How is—"

Her eyes consulted Dwight. His features dropped, the lines of his face dropped, its muscles seemed to sag. A look of suffering was in his eyes.

"She'll never be any better," he said. "I know we've said good-bye to her for the last time."

"Oh, Dwight!" said Lulu.

"She knew it too," he said. "It—it put me out of business, I can tell you. She gave me my start—she took all the care of me—taught me to read—she's the only mother I ever knew—" He stopped, and opened his eyes wide on account of their dimness.

"They said she was like another person while Dwight was there," said Ina, and entered upon a length of particulars, and details of the journey. These details Dwight interrupted: Couldn't Lulu remember that he liked sage on the chops? He could hardly taste it. He had, he said, told her this thirty-seven times. And when she said that she was sorry, "Perhaps you think I'm sage enough," said the witty fellow.

"Dwightie!" said Ina. "Mercy." She shook her head at him. "Now, Di," she went on, keeping the thread all this time. "Tell us your story. About the bag."

"Oh, mamma," said Di, "let me eat my supper."

"And so you shall, darling. Tell it in your own way. Tell us first what you've done since we've been away. Did Mr. Cornish come to see you?"

"Yes," said Di, and flashed a look at Lulu.

But eventually they were back again before that new black bag. And Di would say nothing. She laughed, squirmed, grew irritable, laughed again.

"Lulu!" Ina demanded. "You were with her—where in the world had you been? Why, but you couldn't have been with her—in that dress. And yet I saw you come in the gate together."

"What!" cried Dwight Herbert, drawing down his brows.

"You certainly did not so far forget us, Lulu, as to go on the street in that dress?"

"It's a good dress," Mrs. Bett now said positively. "Of course it's a good dress. Lulie wore it on the street—of course she did. She was gone a long time. I made me a cup o' tea, and *then* she hadn't come."

"Well," said Ina, "I never heard anything like this before. Where were you both?"

One would say that Ina had entered into the family and been born again, identified with each one. Nothing escaped her. Dwight, too, his intimacy was incredible.

"Put an end to this, Lulu," he commanded. "Where were you two—since you make such a mystery?"

Di's look at Lulu was piteous, terrified. Di's fear of her father was now clear to Lulu. And Lulu feared him too. Abruptly she heard herself temporising, for the moment making common cause with Di.

"Oh," she said, "we have a little secret. Can't we have a secret if we want one?"

"Upon my word," Dwight commented, "she has a beautiful secret. I don't know about your secrets, Lulu."

Every time that he did this, that fleet, lifted look of Lulu's seemed to bleed.

"I'm glad for my dinner," remarked Monona at last. "Please excuse me." On that they all rose. Lulu stayed in the kitchen and did her best to make her tasks indefinitely last. She had nearly finished when Di burst in.

"Aunt Lulu, Aunt Lulu!" she cried. "Come in there—come. I can't stand it. What am I going to do?"

"Di, dear," said Lulu. "Tell your mother—you must tell her."

"She'll cry," Di sobbed. "Then she'll tell papa—and he'll never stop talking about it. I know him—every day he'll keep it going. After he scolds me it'll be a joke for months. I'll die—I'll die, Aunt Lulu."

Ina's voice sounded in the kitchen. "What are you two whispering about? I declare, mamma's hurt, Di, at the way you're acting. . . ."

"Let's go out on the porch," said Lulu, and when Di would have escaped, Ina drew her with them, and handled the situation in the only way that she knew how to handle it, by complaining: Well, but what in this world . . .

Lulu threw a white shawl about her blue cotton dress.

"A bridal robe," said Dwight. "How's that, Lulu—what are *you* wearing a bridal robe for—eh?"

She smiled dutifully. There was no need to make him angry, she reflected, before she must. He had not yet gone into the parlour—had not yet asked for his mail.

It was a warm dusk, moonless, windless. The sounds of the village street came in—laughter, a touch at a piano, a chiming clock. Lights starred and quickened in the blurred houses. Footsteps echoed on the board walks. The gate opened. The gloom yielded up Cornish.

Lulu was inordinately glad to see him. To have the strain of the time broken by him was like hearing, on a lonely winter wakening, the clock strike reassuring dawn.

"Lulu," said Dwight low, "your dress. Do go!"

Lulu laughed. "The bridal shawl takes off the curse," she said.

Cornish, in his gentle way, asked about the journey, about the sick woman—and Dwight talked of her again, and this time his voice broke. Di was curiously silent. When Cornish addressed her, she replied simply and directly—the rarest of Di's manners, in fact not Di's manner at all. Lulu spoke not at all—it was enough to have this respite.

After a little the gate opened again. It was Bobby. In the besetting fear that he was leaving Di to face something alone, Bobby had arrived.

And now Di's spirits rose. To her his presence meant repentance, recapitulation. Her laugh rang out, her replies came archly. But Bobby was plainly not playing up. Bobby was, in fact, hardly less than glum. It was Dwight, the irrepressible fellow, who kept the talk going. And it was no less than deft, his continuously displayed ability playfully to pierce Lulu. Some one had "married at the drop of the hat. You know the kind of girl?" And some one "made up a likely story to soothe her own pride—you know how they do that?"

"Well," said Ina, "my part, I think *the* most awful thing is to have somebody one loves keep secrets from one. No wonder folks get crabbed and spiteful with such treatment."

"Mamma!" Monona shouted from her room. "Come and hear me say my prayers!"

Monona entered this request with precision on Ina's nastiest moments, but she always rose, unabashed, and went, motherly and dutiful, to hear devotions, as if that function and the process of living ran their two divided channels.

She had dispatched this errand and was returning when Mrs. Bett crossed the lawn from Grandma Gates's, where the old lady had taken comfort in Mrs. Bett's ministrations for an hour.

"Don't you help me," Mrs. Bett warned them away sharply. "I guess I can help myself yet awhile."

She gained her chair. And still in her momentary rule of attention, she said clearly:

"I got a joke. Grandma Gates says it's all over town Di and

Bobby Larkin eloped off together to-day. *He!*" The last was a single note of laughter, high and brief.

The silence fell.

"What nonsense!" Dwight Herbert said angrily.

But Ina said tensely: "*Is* it nonsense? Haven't I been trying and trying to find out where the black satchel went? Di!"

Di's laughter rose, but it sounded thin and false.

"Listen to that, Bobby," she said. "Listen!"

"That won't do, Di," said Ina. "You can't deceive mamma and don't you try!" Her voice trembled, she was frantic with loving and authentic anxiety, but she was without power, she overshadowed the real gravity of the moment by her indignation.

"Mrs. Deacon—" began Bobby, and stood up, very straight and manly before them all.

But Dwight intervened, Dwight, the father, the master of his house. Here was something requiring him to act. So the father set his face like a mask and brought down his hand on the rail of the porch. It was as if the sound shattered a thousand filaments—where?

"Diana!" his voice was terrible, demanded a response, ravened among them.

"Yes, papa," said Di, very small.

"Answer your mother. Answer *me*. Is there anything to this absurd tale?"

"No, papa," said Di, trembling.

"Nothing whatever?"

"Nothing whatever."

"Can you imagine how such a ridiculous report started?"

"No, papa."

"Very well. Now we know where we are. If anyone hears this report repeated, send them to *me*."

"Well, but that satchel—" said Ina, to whom an idea manifested less as a function than as a leech.

"One moment," said Dwight. "Lulu will of course verify what the child has said."

There had never been an adult moment until that day when Lulu had not instinctively taken the part of the parents, of all parents. Now she saw Dwight's cruelty to her as his cruelty to Di; she saw Ina, herself a child in maternity, as ignorant of how to deal with the moment as was Dwight. She saw Di's falseness partly parented by these parents. She burned at the enormity of Dwight's appeal to her for verification. She threw up her head and no one had ever seen Lulu look like this.

"If you cannot settle this with Di," said Lulu, "you cannot settle it with me."

"A shifty answer," said Dwight. "You have a genius at misrepresenting facts, you know, Lulu."

"Bobby wanted to say something," said Ina, still troubled.

"No, Mrs. Deacon," said Bobby, low. "I have nothing—more to say."

In a little while, when Bobby went away, Di walked with him to the gate. It was as if, the worst having happened to her, she dared everything now.

"Bobby," she said, "you hate a lie. But what else could I do?"

He could not see her, could see only the little moon of her face, blurring.

"And anyhow," said Di, "it wasn't a lie. We *didn't* elope, did we?"

"What do you think I came for to-night?" asked Bobby.

The day had aged him; he spoke like a man. His very voice came gruffly. But she saw nothing, softened to him, yielded, was ready to take his regret that they had not gone on.

"Well, I came for one thing," said Bobby, "to tell you that I couldn't stand for your wanting me to lie to-day. Why, Di—I hate a lie. And now to-night—" He spoke his code almost beautifully. "I'd rather," he said, "they had never let us see each other again than to lose you the way I've lost you now."

"Bobby!"

"It's true. We mustn't talk about it."

"Bobby! I'll go back and tell them all."

"You can't go back," said Bobby. "Not out of a thing like that."

She stood staring after him. She heard some one coming and she turned toward the house, and met Cornish leaving.

"Miss Di," he cried, "if you're going to elope with anybody, remember it's with me!"

Her defence was ready—her laughter rang out so that the departing Bobby might hear.

She came back to the steps and mounted slowly in the lamplight, a little white thing with whom birth had taken exquisite pains.

"If," she said, "if you have any fear that I may ever elope with Bobby Larkin, let it rest. I shall never marry him if he asks me fifty times a day."

"Really, darling?" cried Ina.

"Really and truly," said Di, "and he knows it, too."

Lulu listened and read all.

"I wondered," said Ina pensively, "I wondered if you wouldn't see that Bobby isn't much beside that nice Mr. Cornish!"

When Di had gone upstairs, Ina said to Lulu in a manner of cajoling confidence:

"Sister—" she rarely called her that, "*why* did you and Di have the black bag?"

So that after all it was a relief to Lulu to hear Dwight ask casually:

"By the way, Lulu, haven't I got some mail somewhere about?"

"There are two letters on the parlour table," Lulu answered. To Ina she added: "Let's go in the parlour."

As they passed through the hall, Mrs. Bett was going up the stairs to bed—when she mounted stairs she stooped her shoulders, bunched her extremities, and bent her head. Lulu looked after her, as if she were half minded to claim the protection so long lost.

Dwight lighted the gas. "Better turn down the gas jest a little," said he, tirelessly.

Lulu handed him the two letters. He saw Ninian's writing and looked up, said "A-ha!" and held it while he leisurely read the advertisement of dental furniture, his Ina reading over his shoulder. "A-ha!" he said again, and with designed deliberation turned to Ninian's letter. "An epistle from my dear brother Ninian." The words failed, as he saw the unsealed flap.

"You opened the letter?" he inquired incredulously. Fortunately he had no climaxes of furious calm for high occasions. All had been used on small occasions. "You opened the letter" came in a tone of no deeper horror than "You picked the flower"—once put to Lulu.

She said nothing. As it is impossible to continue looking indignantly at some one who is not looking at you, Dwight turned to Ina, who was horror and sympathy, a nice half and half.

"Your sister has been opening my mail," he said.

"But, Dwight, if it's from Ninian—"

"It is *my* mail," he reminded her. "She had asked me if she might open it. Of course I told her no."

"Well," said Ina practically, "what does he say?"

"I shall open the letter in my own time. My present concern is this disregard of my wishes." His self-control was perfect, ridiculous, devilish. He was self-controlled because thus he could be more effectively cruel than in temper. "What excuse have you to offer?"

Lulu was not looking at him. "None," she said—not defiantly, or ingratiatingly, or fearfully. Merely, "None."

"Why did you do it?"

She smiled faintly and shook her head.

"Dwight," said Ina, reasonably, "she knows what's in it and we don't. Hurry up."

"She is," said Dwight, after a pause, "an ungrateful woman."

He opened the letter, saw the clipping, the avowal, with its facts.

"A-ha!" said he. "So after having been absent with my brother for a month, you find that you were *not* married to him."

Lulu spoke her exceeding triumph.

"You see, Dwight," she said, "he told the truth. He had another wife. He didn't just leave me."

Dwight instantly cried: "But this seems to me to make you considerably worse off than if he had."

"Oh, no," Lulu said serenely. "No. Why," she said, "you know how it all came about. He—he was used to thinking of his wife as dead. If he hadn't—hadn't liked me, he wouldn't have told me. You see that, don't you?"

Dwight laughed. "That your apology?" he asked.

She said nothing.

"Look here, Lulu," he went on, "this is a bad business. The less you say about it the better, for all our sakes—*you* see that, don't you?"

"See that? Why, no. I wanted you to write to him so I could tell the truth. You said I mustn't tell the truth till I had the proofs. . . ."

"Tell who?"

"Tell everybody. I want them to know."

"Then you care nothing for our feelings in this matter?"

She looked at him now. "Your feeling?"

"It's nothing to you that we have a brother who's a bigamist?"

"But it's me—it's me."

"You! You're completely out of it. Just let it rest as it is and it'll drop."

"I want the people to know the truth," Lulu said.

"But it's nobody's business but our business! I take it you don't intend to sue Ninian?"

"Sue him? Oh no!"

"Then, for all our sakes, let's drop the matter."

Lulu had fallen in one of her old attitudes, tense, awkward, her hands awkwardly placed, her feet twisted. She kept putting a lock back of her ear, she kept swallowing.

"Tell you, Lulu," said Dwight. "Here are three of us. Our interests are the same in this thing—only Ninian is our relative and he's nothing to you now. Is he?"

"Why, no," said Lulu in surprise.

"Very well. Let's have a vote. Your snap judgment is to tell this disgraceful fact broadcast. Mine is, least said, soonest mended. What do you say, Ina—considering Di and all?"

"Oh, goodness," said Ina, "if we get mixed up with bigamy, we'll never get away from it. Why, I wouldn't have it told for worlds."

Still in that twisted position, Lulu looked up at her. Her straying hair, her parted lips, her lifted eyes were singularly pathetic.

"My poor, poor sister!" Ina said. She struck together her little plump hands. "Oh, Dwight—when I think of it: What have I done—what have *we* done that I should have a good, kind, loving husband—be so protected, so loved, when other women . . . Darling!" she sobbed, and drew near to Lulu. "You *know* how sorry I am—we all are. . . ."

Lulu stood up. The white shawl slipped to the floor. Her hands were stiffly joined.

"Then," she said, "give me the only thing I've got—that's my pride. My pride—that he didn't want to get rid of me."

They stared at her. "What about *my* pride?" Dwight called to her, as across great distances. "Do you think I want everybody to know my brother did a thing like that?"

"You can't help that," said Lulu.

"But I want you to help it. I want you to promise me that you won't shame us like this before all our friends."

"You want me to promise what?"

"I want you—I ask you," Dwight said with an effort, "to promise me that you will keep this, with us—a family secret."

"No!" Lulu cried. "No. I won't do it! I won't do it! I won't do it!"

It was like some crude chant, knowing only two tones. She threw out her hands, her wrists long and dark on her blue skirt.

"Can't you understand anything?" she asked. "I've lived here all my life—on your money. I've not been strong enough to work, they say—well, but I've been strong enough to be a hired girl in your house—and I've been glad to pay for my keep. . . . But there wasn't anything about it I liked. Nothing about being here that I liked. . . . Well, then I got a little something, same as other folks.

I thought I was married and I went off on the train and he bought me things and I saw the different towns. And then it was all a mistake. I didn't have any of it. I came back here and went into your kitchen again—I don't know why I came back. I s'pose because I'm most thirty-four and new things ain't so easy any more—but what have I got or what'll I ever have? And now you want to put on to me having folks look at me and think he run off and left me, and having 'em all wonder. . . . I can't stand it. I can't stand it. I can't. . . ."

"You'd rather they'd know he fooled you, when he had another wife?" Dwight sneered.

"Yes! Because he wanted me. How do I know—maybe he wanted me only just because he was lonesome, the way I was. I don't care why! And I won't have folks think he went and left me."

"That," said Dwight, "is a wicked vanity."

"That's the truth. Well, why can't they know the truth?"

"And bring disgrace on us all."

"It's me—it's me—" Lulu's individualism strove against that terrible tribal sense, was shattered by it.

"It's all of us!" Dwight boomed. "It's Di."

"Di?" He had Lulu's eyes now.

"Why, it's chiefly on Di's account that I'm talking," said Dwight.

"How would it hurt Di?"

"To have a thing like that in the family? Well, can't you see how it'd hurt her?"

"Would it, Ina? Would it hurt Di?"

"Why, it would shame her—embarrass her—make people wonder what kind of stock she came from—oh," Ina sobbed, "my pure little girl!"

"Hurt her prospects, of course," said Dwight. "Anybody could see that."

"I s'pose it would," said Lulu.

She clasped her arms tightly, awkwardly, and stepped about the floor, her broken shoes showing beneath her cotton skirt.

"When a family once get talked about for any reason—" said Ina and shuddered.

"I'm talked about now!"

"But nothing that you could help. If he got tired of you, you couldn't help that." This misstep was Dwight's.

"No," Lulu said, "I couldn't help that. And I couldn't help his other wife, either."

"Bigamy," said Dwight, "that's a crime."

"I've done no crime," said Lulu.

"Bigamy," said Dwight, "disgraces everybody it touches."

"Even Di," Lulu said.

"Lulu," said Dwight, "on Di's account will you promise us to let this thing rest with us three?"

"I s'pose so," said Lulu quietly.

"You will?"

"I s'pose so."

Ina sobbed: "Thank you, thank you, Lulu. This makes up for everything."

Lulu was thinking: "Di has a hard enough time as it is." Aloud she said: "I told Mr. Cornish, but he won't tell."

"I'll see to that," Dwight graciously offered.

"Goodness," Ina said, "so he knows. Well, that settles—" She said no more.

"You'll be happy to think you've done this for us, Lulu," said Dwight.

"I s'pose so," said Lulu.

Ina, pink from her little gust of sobbing, went to her, kissed her, her trim tan tailor suit against Lulu's blue cotton.

"My sweet, self-sacrificing sister," she murmured.

"Oh stop that!" Lulu said.

Dwight took her hand, lying limply in his. "I can now," he said, "overlook the matter of the letter."

Lulu drew back. She put her hair behind her ears, swallowed, and cried out.

"Don't you go around pitying me! I'll have you know I'm glad the whole thing happened!"

Cornish had ordered six new copies of a popular song. He knew that it was popular because it was called so in a Chicago paper. When the six copies arrived with a danseuse on the covers he read the "words," looked wistfully at the symbols which shut him out, and felt well pleased.

"Got up quite attractive," he thought, and fastened the six copies in the window of his music store.

It was not yet nine o'clock of a vivid morning. Cornish had his floor and sidewalk sprinkled, his red and blue plush piano spreads dusted. He sat at a folding table well back in the store, and opened a law book.

For half an hour he read. Then he found himself looking off the page, stabbed by a reflection which always stabbed him anew: Was he really getting anywhere with his law? And where did he really hope to get? Of late when he awoke at night this question had stood by the cot, waiting.

The cot had appeared there in the back of the music store, behind a dark sateen curtain with too few rings on the wire. How little else was in there, nobody knew. But those passing in the late evening saw the blur of his kerosene lamp behind that curtain and were smitten by a realistic illusion of personal loneliness.

It was behind that curtain that these unreasoning questions usually attacked him, when his giant, wavering shadow had died upon the wall and the faint smell of the extinguished lamp went with him to his bed; or when he waked before any sign of dawn. In the mornings all was cheerful and wonted—the question had not before attacked him among his red and blue plush spreads, his golden oak and ebony cases, of a sunshiny morning.

A step at his door set him flying. He wanted passionately to sell a piano.

"Well!" he cried, when he saw his visitor.

It was Lulu, in her dark red suit and her tilted hat.

"Well!" she also said, and seemed to have no idea of saying anything else. Her excitement was so obscure that he did not discern it.

"You're out early," said he, participating in the village chorus of this bright challenge at this hour.

"Oh, no," said Lulu.

He looked out the window, pretending to be caught by something passing, leaned to see it the better.

"Oh, how'd you get along last night?" he asked, and wondered why he had not thought to say it before.

"All right, thank you," said Lulu.

"Was he—about the letter, you know?"

"Yes," she said, "but that didn't matter. You'll be sure," she added, "not to say anything about what was in the letter?"

"Why, not till you tell me I can," said Cornish, "but won't everybody know now?"

"No," Lulu said.

At this he had no more to say, and feeling his speculation in his eyes, dropped them to a piano scarf from which he began flicking invisible specks.

"I came to tell you good-bye," Lulu said.

"Good-bye!"

"Yes. I'm going off—for a while. My satchel's in the bakery—I had my breakfast in the bakery."

"Say!" Cornish cried warmly, "then everything *wasn't* all right last night?"

"As right as it can ever be with me," she told him. "Oh, yes. Dwight forgave me."

"Forgave you!"

She smiled, and trembled.

"Look here," said Cornish, "you come here and sit down and tell me about this."

He led her to the folding table, as the only social spot in that vast area of his, seated her in the one chair, and for himself brought up a piano stool. But after all she told him nothing. She merely took the comfort of his kindly indignation.

"It came out all right," she said only. "But I won't stay there any more. I can't do that."

"Then what are you going to do?"

"In Millton yesterday," she said, "I saw an advertisement in the hotel—they wanted a chambermaid."

"Oh, Miss Bett!" he cried. At that name she flushed. "Why," said Cornish, "you must have been coming from Millton yesterday when I saw you. I noticed Miss Di had her bag—" He stopped, stared. "You brought her back!" he deduced everything.

"Oh!" said Lulu. "Oh, no—I mean—"

"I heard about the eloping again this morning," he said. "That's just what you did—you brought her back."

"You mustn't tell that! You won't? You won't!"

"No. 'Course not." He mulled it. "You tell me this: Do they know? I mean about your going after her?"

"No."

"You never told!"

"They don't know she went."

"That's a funny thing," he blurted out, "for you not to tell her folks—I mean, right off. Before last night . . ."

"You don't know them. Dwight'd never let up on that—he'd *joke* her about it after a while."

"But it seems—"

"Ina'd talk about disgracing *her.* They wouldn't know what to do. There's no sense in telling them. They aren't a mother and father," Lulu said.

Cornish was not accustomed to deal with so much reality. But Lulu's reality he could grasp.

"You're a trump anyhow," he affirmed.

"Oh, no," said Lulu modestly.

Yes, she was. He insisted upon it.

"By George," he exclaimed, "you don't find very many *married* women with as good sense as you've got."

At this, just as he was agonising because he had seemed to refer to the truth that she was, after all, not married, at this Lulu laughed in some amusement, and said nothing.

"You've been a jewel in their home all right," said Cornish. "I bet they'll miss you if you do go."

"They'll miss my cooking," Lulu said without bitterness.

"They'll miss more than that, I know. I've often watched you there—"

"You have?" It was not so much pleasure as passionate gratitude which lighted her eyes.

"You made the whole place," said Cornish.

"You don't mean just the cooking?"

"No, no. I mean—well, that first night when you played croquet. I felt at home when you came out."

That look of hers, rarely seen, which was no less than a look of loveliness, came now to Lulu's face. After a pause she said:

"I never had but one compliment before that wasn't for my cooking." She seemed to feel that she must confess to that one. "He told me I done my hair up nice." She added conscientiously: "That was after I took notice how the ladies in Savannah, Georgia, done up theirs."

"Well, well," said Cornish only.

"Well," said Lulu, "I must be going now. I wanted to say good-bye to you—and there's one or two other places. . . ."

"I hate to have you go," said Cornish, and tried to add something. "I hate to have you go," was all that he could find to add.

Lulu rose. "Oh, well," was all that she could find.

They shook hands, Lulu laughing a little. Cornish followed her to the door. He had begun on "Look here, I wish . . ." when Lulu said "good-bye," and paused, wishing intensely to know what he would have said. But all that he said was: "Good-bye. I wish you weren't going."

"So do I," said Lulu, and went, still laughing.

Cornish saw her red dress vanish from his door, flash by his window, her head averted. And there settled upon him a depression out of all proportion to the slow depression of his days. This was more—it assailed him, absorbed him.

He stood staring out the window. Some one passed with a greeting of which he was conscious too late to return. He wandered back down the store and his pianos looked back at him like strangers. Down there was the green curtain which screened his home life. He suddenly hated that green curtain. He hated this whole place. For the first time it occurred to him that he hated Warbleton.

He came back to his table, and sat down before his lawbook. But he sat, chin on chest, regarding it. No . . . no escape that way. . . .

A step at the door and he sprang up. It was Lulu, coming toward him, her face unsmiling but somehow quite lighted. In her hand was a letter.

"See," she said. "At the office was this. . . ."

She thrust in his hand the single sheet. He read:

> ". . . just wanted you to know you're actually rid of me. I've heard from her, in Brazil. She ran out of money and thought of me, and her lawyer wrote to me. . . . I've never been any good—Dwight would tell you that if his pride would let him tell the truth once in a while. But there ain't anything in my life makes me feel as bad as this. . . . I s'pose you couldn't understand and I don't myself. . . . Only the sixteen years keeping still made me think she was gone sure . . . but you were so downright good, that's what was the worst . . . do you see what I want to say . . .

Cornish read it all and looked at Lulu. She was grave and in her eyes there was a look of dignity such as he had never seen them wear. Incredible dignity.

"He didn't lie to get rid of me—and she was alive, just as he thought she might be," she said.

"I'm glad," said Cornish.

"Yes," said Lulu "He isn't quite so bad as Dwight tried to make him out."

It was not of this that Cornish had been thinking.

"Now you're free," he said.

"Oh, that . . ." said Lulu.

She replaced her letter in its envelope. "Now I'm really going," she said. "Good-bye for sure this time. . . ."

Her words trailed away. Cornish had laid his hand on her arm.

"Don't say good-bye," he said.

"It's late," she said, "I—"

"Don't you go," said Cornish.

She looked at him mutely.

"Do you think you could possibly stay here with me?"

"Oh!" said Lulu, like no word.

He went on, not looking at her. "I haven't got anything. I guess maybe you've heard something about a little something I'm supposed to inherit. Well, it's only five hundred dollars."

His look searched her face, but she hardly heard what he was saying.

"That little Warden house—it don't cost much—you'd be surprised. Rent, I mean. I can get it now. I went and looked at it the other day, but then I didn't think—" he caught himself on that. "It don't cost near as much as this store. We could furnish up the parlour with pianos—"

He was startled by that "we," and began again:

"That is, if you could ever think of such a thing as marrying me."

"But," said Lulu. "You *know!* Why, don't the disgrace—"

"What disgrace?" asked Cornish.

"Oh," she said, "you—you—"

"There's only this about that," said he. "Of course, if you loved him very much, then I'd ought not to be talking this way to you. But I didn't think—"

"You didn't think what?"

"That you did care so very much—about him. I don't know why."

She said: "I wanted somebody of my own. That's the reason I done what I done. I know that now."

"I figured that way," said Cornish.

They dismissed it. But now he brought to bear something which he saw that she should know.

"Look here," he said, "I'd ought to tell you. I'm—I'm awful lonesome myself. This is no place to live. And I guess living so is one reason why I want to get married. I want some kind of a home."

He said it as a confession. She accepted it as a reason.

"Of course," she said.

"I ain't never lived what you might say private," said Cornish.

"I've lived too private," Lulu said.

"Then there's another thing." This was harder to tell her. "I—I don't believe I'm ever going to be able to do a thing with law."

"I don't see," said Lulu, "how anybody does."

"I'm not much good in a business way," he owned, with a faint laugh. "Sometimes I think," he drew down his brows, "that I may never be able to make any money."

She said: "Lots of men don't."

"Could you risk it with me?" Cornish asked her. "There's nobody I've seen," he went on gently, "that I like as much as I do you. I—I was engaged to a girl once, but we didn't get along. I guess if you'd be willing to try me, we would get along."

Lulu said: "I thought it was Di that you—"

"Miss Di? Why," said Cornish, "she's a little kid. And," he added, "she's a little liar."

"But I'm going on thirty-four."

"So am I!"

"Isn't there somebody—"

"Look here. Do you like me?"

"Oh, yes!"

"Well enough—"

"It's you I was thinking of," said Lulu. "I'd be all right."

"Then!" Cornish cried, and he kissed her.

"And now," said Dwight, "nobody must mind if I hurry a little wee bit. I've got something on."

He and Ina and Monona were at dinner. Mrs. Bett was in her room. Di was not there.

"Anything about Lulu?" Ina asked.

"Lulu?" Dwight stared. "Why should I have anything to do about Lulu?"

"Well, but, Dwight—we've got to do something."

"As I told you this morning," he observed, "we shall do nothing. Your sister is of age—I don't know about the sound mind, but she is certainly of age. If she chooses to go away, she is free to go where she will."

"Yes, but, Dwight, where has she gone? Where could she go? Where—"

"You are a question-box," said Dwight playfully. "A question-box."

Ina had burned her plump wrist on the oven. She lifted her arm and nursed it.

"I'm certainly going to miss her if she stays away very long," she remarked.

"You should be sufficient unto your little self," said Dwight.

"That's all right," said Ina, "except when you're getting dinner."

"I want some crust coffee," announced Monona firmly.

"You'll have nothing of the sort," said Ina. "Drink your milk."

"As I remarked," Dwight went on, "I'm in a tiny wee bit of a hurry."

"Well, why don't you say what for?" his Ina asked.

She knew that he wanted to be asked, and she was sufficiently willing to play his games, and besides she wanted to know. But she *was* hot.

"I am going," said Dwight, "to take Grandma Gates out in a wheel-chair, for an hour."

"Where did you get a wheel-chair, for mercy sakes?"

"Borrowed it from the railroad company," said Dwight, with the triumph peculiar to the resourceful man. "Why I never did it before, I can't imagine. There that chair's been in the depot ever since I can remember—saw it every time I took the train—and yet I never once thought of grandma."

"My, Dwight," said Ina, "how good you are!"

"Nonsense!" said he.

"Well, you are. Why don't I send her over a baked apple? Monona, you take Grandma Gates a baked apple—no. You shan't go till you drink your milk."

"I don't want it."

"Drink it or mamma won't let you go."

Monona drank it, made a piteous face, took the baked apple, ran.

"The apple isn't very good," said Ina, "but it shows my good will."

"Also," said Dwight, "it teaches Monona a life of thoughtfulness for others."

"That's what I always think," his Ina said.

"Can't you get mother to come out?" Dwight inquired.

"I had so much to do getting dinner onto the table, I didn't try," Ina confessed.

"You didn't have to try," Mrs. Bett's voice sounded. "I was coming when I got rested up."

She entered, looking vaguely about. "I want Lulie," she said, and the corners of her mouth drew down. She ate her dinner cold, appeased in vague areas by such martyrdom. They were still at table when the front door opened.

"Monona hadn't ought to use the front door so common," Mrs. Bett complained.

But it was not Monona. It was Lulu and Cornish.

"Well!" said Dwight, tone curving downward.

"Well!" said Ina, in replica.

"Lulie!" said Mrs. Bett, and left her dinner, and went to her daughter and put her hands upon her.

"We wanted to tell you first," Cornish said. "We've just got married."

"For*ever*more!" said Ina.

"What's this?" Dwight sprang to his feet. "You're joking!" he cried with hope.

"No," Cornish said soberly. "We're married—just now. Methodist parsonage. We've had our dinner," he added hastily.

"Where'd you have it?" Ina demanded, for no known reason.

"The bakery," Cornish replied, and flushed.

"In the dining-room part," Lulu added.

Dwight's sole emotion was his indignation.

"What on earth did you do it for?" he put it to them. "Married in a bakery—"

No, no. They explained it again. Neither of them, they said, wanted the fuss of a wedding.

Dwight recovered himself in a measure. "I'm not surprised, after all," he said. "Lulu usually marries in this way."

Mrs. Bett patted her daughter's arm. "Lulie," she said, "why, Lulie. You ain't been and got married twice, have you? After waitin' so long?"

"Don't be disturbed, Mother Bett," Dwight cried. "She wasn't married that first time, if you remember. No marriage about it!"

Ina's little shriek sounded.

"Dwight!" she cried. "Now everybody'll have to know that. You'll have to tell about Ninian now—and his other wife!"

Standing between her mother and Cornish, an arm of each about her, Lulu looked across at Ina and Dwight, and they all saw in her face a horrified realisation.

"Ina!" she said. "Dwight! You *will* have to tell now, won't you? Why, I never thought of that."

At this Dwight sneered, was sneering still as he went to give Grandma Gates her ride in the wheel-chair and as he stooped with patient kindness to tuck her in.

The street door was closed. If Mrs. Bett was peeping through the blind, no one saw her. In the pleasant mid-day light under the maples, Mr. and Mrs. Neil Cornish were hurrying toward the railway station.

STORIES

Dream

When a house in the neighborhood has been vacant for two years, and all of a sudden the neighborhood sees furniture being moved into that house, excitement, as Silas Sykes says, reigns supreme and more than supreme.

And so it did in Friendship Village when the Oldmoxon House got a new tenant, unbeknownst. The excitement was specially strained because the reason Oldmoxon House had stood vacant so long was the rent. And whoever had agreed to the Twenty Dollars was going to be, we all felt, and as Mis' Sykes herself put it, "a distinct addition to Friendship Village society."

It was she gave me the news, being the Sykeses are the Oldmoxon House's nearest neighbors. I hurried right over to her house—it was summer-warm and you just ached for an excuse to be out in it, anyway. We drew some rockers onto her front porch where we could get a good view. The Oldmoxon double front doors stood open, and the things were being set inside.

"Serves me right not to know who it is," says Mis' Sykes. "I see men working there yesterday, and I never went over to inquire what they were doing."

"A body can't do everything that's expected of them," says I, soothing.

"Won't it be nice," says Mis' Sykes, dreamy, "to have that house open again, and folks going and coming, and maybe parties?" It was then the piano came out of the van, and she gave her ultimatum. "Whoever it is," she says, pointing eloquent, "will be a distinct addition to Friendship Village society."

There wasn't a soul in sight that seemed to be doing the directing, so pretty soon Mis' Sykes says, uneasy:

"I don't know—would it seem—how would it be—well, wouldn't it be taking a neighborly interest to step over and question the vans a little?"

And we both of us thought it would be in order, so we did step right over to inquire.

Being the vans had come out from the City, we didn't find out much except our new neighbor's name: Burton Fernandez.

"The Burton Fernandezes," says Mis' Sykes, as we picked our way back. "I guess when we write that name to our friends in our letters, they won't think we live in the woods any more. Calliope," she says, "it come to me this: Don't you think it would be real nice to get them up a reception-surprise, and all go there some night as soon as they get settled, and take our own refreshments, and get acquainted all at once, instead of using up time to call, individual?"

"Land, yes," I says, "I'd like to do that to every neighbor that comes into town. But you—" says I, hesitating, to her that was usually so exclusive she counted folks's grand-folks on her fingers before she would go to call on them, "what makes you—"

"Oh," says Mis' Sykes, "you can't tell me. Folks's individualities is expressed in folks's furniture. You can't tell me that, with those belongings, we can go wrong in our judgment."

"Well," I says, "*I* can't go wrong, because I can't think of anything that'd make me give them the cold shoulder. That's another comfort about being friends to everybody—you don't have to decide which ones you want to know."

"You're so queer, Calliope," says Mis' Sykes, tolerant. "You miss all the satisfaction of being exclusive. And you can't *afford* not to be."

"Mebbe not," says I, "mebbe not. But I'm willing to try it. Hang the expense!" says I.

Mis' Sykes didn't waste a day on her reception-surprise. I heard of it right off from Mis' Holcomb and Mis' Toplady and two-three more. They were all willing enough, not only because any excitement in the village is like a personal present to all of us, but because Mis' Sykes was interested. She's got a real gift for making folks think her way is the way. She's a real leader. Everybody wears a straw hat contented till, somewheres near November, Mis' Sykes flams out in felt, and then you begin right off to feel shabby in your straw, though new from the store that Spring.

"It does seem like rushing things a little, though," says Mis' Holcomb to me, very confidential, the next day.

"Not for me," I says. "I been vaccinated."

"What do you mean?" says she.

"Not even the small-pox can make me snub them," I explains.

"Yes, but Calliope," says Mis' Toplady in a whisper, "suppose it should turn out to be one of them awful places we read about. They have good furniture."

"Well," says I, "in that case, if thirty to forty of us went in with our baskets, real friendly, and done it often enough, I bet we'd either drive them out or turn them into better neighbors. Where's the harm?"

"Calliope," says Mame Holcomb, "don't you draw the line *nowheres*?"

"Yes," I says, mournful. "Them on Mars won't speak to me—yet. But short of Mars—no. I have no lines up."

We heard from the servant that came down on Tuesday and began cleaning and settling, that the family would arrive on Friday. We didn't get much out of him—a respectable-seeming colored man but reticent, very. The fact that the family servant was a man finished Mis' Sykes. She had had a strong leaning, but now she was bent, visible. And with an item that appeared Thursday night in the Friendship Village *Evening Daily,* she toppled complete.

"Professor and Mrs. Burton Fernandez," the *Supper Table Jottings* said, "are expected Friday to take possession of Oldmoxon House, 506 Daphne Street. Professor Fernandez is to be engaged for some time in some academic and scholastic work in the City. Welcome, Neighbors."

"Let's have our reception-surprise for them Saturday night," says Mis' Sykes, as soon as she had read the item. "Then we can make them right at home, first thing, and they won't need to tramp into church, feeling strange, Next-day morning."

"Go on—do it," says I, affable.

Mis' Sykes ain't one to initiate civic, but she's the one to initiate festive, every time.

Mis' Holcomb and Mis' Toplady and me agreed to bake the cakes, and Mis' Sykes was to furnish the lemonade, being her husband keeps the Post-office store, and what she gets, she gets wholesale. And Mis' Sykes let it be known around that on Saturday night we were all to drop into her house, and go across the street together, with our baskets, to put in a couple of hours at our new neighbors', and make them feel at home. And everybody was looking forward to it.

I've got some hyacinth bulbs along by my side fence that get up and come out, late April and early May, and all but speak to you. And it happened when I woke up Friday morning they looked so lovely, I couldn't resist them. I had to take some of them up, and set them out in pots and carry them around to a few. About noon I was going along the street with one to take to an old colored washer-woman I know, that never does see much that's beautiful but the sky; but when I got in front of Oldmoxon House, a thought met me.

"To-day's the day they come," I said to myself. "Be kind of nice to have a sprig of something there to welcome them."

So my feet turned me right in, like your feet do sometimes, and I rang the front bell.

"Here," says I, to that colored servant that opened the door, "is a posy I thought your folks might like to see waiting for them."

He started to speak, but somebody else spoke first.

"How friendly!" said a nice-soft voice—I noticed the voice particular. "Let me thank her."

There came out from the shadow of the hall, a woman—the one with the lovely voice.

"I am Mrs. Fernandez—this is good of you," she said, and put out her hands for the plant.

I gave it to her, and I don't believe I looked surprised, any more than when I first saw the pictures of the Disciples, that the artist had painted their skin dark, like it must have been. Mrs. Fernandez was dark too. But her people had come, not from Asia, but from Africa.

Like a flash, I saw what this was going to mean in the village. And in the second that I stood there, without time to think it through, something told me to go in, and try to get some idea of what was going to be what.

"May I come inside now I'm here?" I says.

She took me into the room that was the most settled of any. The piano was there, and a good many books on their shelves. As I remember back now, I must just have stood and stared at them, for impressions were chasing each other across my head like waves on a heaving sea. No less than that, and mebbe more.

"I was trying to decide where to put the pictures," she said. "Then we shall have everything settled before my husband gets home to-morrow."

We talked about the pictures—they were photographs of Venice and of Spain. Then we talked about the garden, and whether it was too late for her to plant much, and I promised her some aster plants. Then I saw a photograph of a young girl—it was her daughter, in Chicago University, who would be coming home to spend the Summer. Her son had been studying to be a surgeon, she said.

"My husband," she told me, "has some work to do in the library in the City. We tried to live there—but we couldn't bear it."

"I'm glad you came here," I told her. "It's as nice a little place as any."

"I suppose so," she says only. "As nice as—any."

I don't think I stayed half an hour. But when I came out of there I walked away from Oldmoxon House not sensing much of anything except a kind of singing thanksgiving. I had never known anything of her people except the kind like our colored wash-woman. I knew about the negro colleges and all, but I guess

I never thought about the folks that must be graduating from them. I'd always thought that there might be somebody like Mis' Fernandez, sometime, a long way off, when the Lord and us his helpers got around to it. And here already it was true of some of them. It was like seeing the future come true right in my face.

When I shut the gate of Oldmoxon House, I see Mis' Sykes peeking out her front door, and motioning to me. And at the sight of her, that I hadn't thought of since I went into that house, I had all I could do to keep from laughing and crying together, till the street rang with me. I crossed over and went in her gate; and her eye-brows were all cocked inquiring to take in the news.

"Go on," she says, "and tell me all there is to tell. Is it all so—the name—and her husband—and all?"

"Yes," I says, "it's all so."

"I knew it when I see her come," says Mis' Sykes. "Her hat and her veil and her simple, good-cut black clothes—you can't fool me on a lady."

"No," I says. "You can't fool me, either."

"Well now," says Mis' Sykes, "there's nothing to hinder our banging right ahead with our plan for to-morrow night, is there?"

"Nothing whatever," I says, "to hinder me."

Mis' Sykes jerked herself around and looked at me irritable.

"Why don't you volunteer?" says she. "I hate to dig the news out of anybody with the can-opener."

I'd have given a good deal to feel that I didn't have to tell her, but just let her go ahead with the reception surprise. I knew, though, that I ought to tell her, not only because I knew her through and through, but because I couldn't count on the village. We're real democratic in the things we know about, but let a new situation stick up its head and we bound to the other side, automatic.

"Mis' Sykes," I says, "everything that we'd thought of our new neighbor is true. *Also,* she's going to be a new experience for us in a way we hadn't thought of. She's dark-skinned."

"A brunette," says Mis' Sykes. "I see that through her veil—what of it?"

"Nothing—nothing at all," says I. "You noticed then, that she's colored?"

I want to laugh yet, every time I think how Mis' Postmaster Sykes looked at me.

"Colored!" she says. "You mean—you can't mean—"

"No," I says, "nothing dangerous. It's going to give us a chance to see that what we've always said could be true sometime, away far off, is true of some of them now."

Mis' Sykes sprang up and began walking the floor.

"A family like that in Oldmoxon House—and my nearest neighbors," says she, wild. "It's outrageious—outrageious."

I don't use my words very good, but I know better than to say "outrageious." I don't know but it was her pronouncing it that way, in such a cause, that made me so mad.

"Mis' Sykes," I says, "Mis' Fernandez has got a better education than either you or I. She's a graduate of a Southern college, and her two children have been to colleges that you and I have never seen the inside of and never will. And her husband is a college professor, up here to study for a degree that I don't even know what the letters stands for. In what," says I, "consists your and my superiority to that woman?"

"My gracious," says Mis' Sykes, "ain't you got no sense of fitness to you. Ain't she black?"

"Her skin ain't the same color as ours, you're saying," I says. "Don't it seem to you that that reason had ought to make a cat laugh?"

Mis' Sykes fair wheeled on me. "Calliope Marsh," says she, "the way you set your opinions against established notions is an insult to your kind."

"Established notions," I says over after her. "'Established notions.' That's just it. And who is it, of us two, that's being insulting to their kind now, Mis' Sykes?"

She was looking out the window, with her lips close-pressed and a thought between her narrowed eye-lids.

"I'll rejoin 'em—or whatever it is you call it," she says. "I'll rejoin 'em from living in that house next to me."

"Mis' Sykes!" says I. "But their piano and their book-cases and their name are just the same as yesterday. You know yourself how you said folks's furniture expressed them. And it does—so be they ain't using left-overs the way I am. I tell you, I've talked with her, and I know. Or rather I kept still while she told me things about Venice and Granada where she'd been and I hadn't. You've got all you thought you had in that house, and education besides. Are you the Christian woman, Mis' Sykes, to turn your nose up at them?"

"Don't throw my faith in my face," says she, irritable.

"Well," I says, "I won't twit on facts. But anybody'd think the Golden Rule's fitted neat onto some folks to deal with, and is left flap at loose ends for them that don't match our skins. Is that sense, or ain't it?"

"It ain't the skin," she says. "Don't keep harping on that. It's them. They're different by nature."

Then she says the great, grand motto of the little thin slice of the human race that's been changed into superiority.

"You can't change human nature!" says she, ticking it out like a clock.

"Can't you?" says I. "*Can't* you? I'm interested. If that was true, you and I would be swinging by our tails, this minute, sociable, from your clothes-line."

By this time she didn't hear anything anybody said back—she'd got to that point in the argument.

"If," she says positive, "if the Lord had intended dark-skinned folks to be different from what they are, he'd have seen to it by now."

I shifted with her obliging.

"Then," says I, "take the Fernandez family, in the Oldmoxon House. They're different. They're more different than you and I are. What you going to do about it?"

Mis' Sykes stamped her foot. "How do you know," she says, "that the Lord intended them to be educated? Tell me that!"

I sat looking down at her three-ply Ingrain carpet for a minute or two. Then I got up, and asked her for her chocolate frosting receipt.

"I'm going to use that on my cake for to-morrow night," I says. "And do you want me to help with the rest of the telephoning?"

"What do you mean?" she says, frigid. "You don't think for a minute I'm going on with that, I hope?"

"On with it?" I says. "Didn't you tell me you had the arrangements about all made?"

She sunk back, loose in her chair. "I shall be the Laughing Stock,—the Laughing Stock," she says, looking wild and glazed.

"Yes," says I, deliberate, determined and serene, "they'll say you were going to dance around and cater to this family because they've moved into the Oldmoxon House. They'll say you wanted to make sure, right away, to get in with them. They'll repeat what you've been saying about the elegant furniture, in good taste. And about the academic and scholastic work being done.

And about these folks being a distinct addition to Friendship Village society—"

"Don't, Calliope—oh, don't!" said Mis' Sykes, faint.

"Well, then," I says, getting up to leave, "go on ahead and act neighborly to them, the once, and decide later about keeping it up, as you would with anybody else."

It kind of swept over me—here we were, standing there, bickering and haggling, when out there on the planet that lay around Daphne Street were loose ends of creation to catch up and knit in.

"My gracious," I says, "I ain't saying they're all all right, am I? But I'm saying that as fast as those that try to grow, stick up their heads, it's the business of us that tootle for democracy, and for evolution, to help them on."

She looked at me, pitying.

"It's all so much bigger than that, Calliope," she says.

"True," says I, "for if some of them stick up their heads, it proves that more of them could—if we didn't stomp 'em down."

I got out in the air of the great, gold May day, that was like another way of life, leading up from our way. I took in a long breath of it—and that always helps me to see things big.

"One Spring," I says, "One world—one God—one life—one future. Wouldn't you think we could match ourselves up?"

But when I got in my little house, I looked around on the homely inside of it—that always helps me to think how much better things can be, when we really know how. And I says:

"Oh, God, we here in America got up a terrible question for you to help us settle, didn't we? Well, *help* us! And help us to see, whatever's the way to settle anything, that giving the cold shoulder and the uplifted nose to any of the creatures you've made ain't the way to settle *nothing*. Amen."

❧

Next morning I was standing in my door-way, breathing in the fresh, gold air, when in at the gate came that colored man of Mis' Fernandez's, and he had a big bouquet of roses. Not roses like we in the village often see. They were green-house bred.

"Mis' Fernandez's son done come home las' night and bring 'em," says the man.

"Her son," I says, "from college?"

"No'm," says the man. "F'om the war."

"From the what?" I says.

"F'om the war," he says over. "F'om U'pe."

He must have thought I was crazy. For a minute I stared at him, then I says "Glory be!" and I began to laugh. Then I told him to tell Mis' Fernandez that I'd be over in half an hour to thank her myself for the flowers, and in half an hour I was going up to her front door. I had to make sure.

"Your son," I says, forgetting all about the roses, "he's in the American army?"

"He was," she said. "He fought in France for eighteen months. Now he has been discharged."

"Oh," I says to myself, "that arranges everything. It must."

"Perhaps you will let me tell you," she said. "He comes back to us wearing the cross of war."

"The cross of war!" I cried. "That they give when folks save folks in battle?" I said it just like saving folks is the principal business of it all.

"My son did save a wounded officer in No-man's land," she told me. "The officer—he was a white man."

"Oh," I says, and I couldn't say another word till I managed to ask her if her son had been in the draft.

"No," she said. "He volunteered April 7, 1917."

It wasn't until I got out in the street that I remembered I hadn't thanked her for the roses at all. But there wasn't time to think of that.

I headed straight for Mis' Silas Sykes. She looked awful bad, and I don't think probably she'd slept a wink all night. I ask' her casual how the reception was coming on, and she kind of began to cry.

"I don't know what you hector me for like this," she says. "Ain't it enough that I've got to call folks up to-day and tell them I've made a fool of myself?"

"Not yet," I says. "Not yet you ain't made one of yourself, Mis' Sykes. That's to come, if any. It is hard," I says, "to do the particular thing you'll have to do. There's them," I says crafty, "as'll gloat."

"I thought about them all night long," she says, her breath showing through her words.

"Then think no more, Mis' Sykes," I says, "because there's a reason over there in that house why we should go ahead with our plan—and it's a reason you can't get around."

She looked at me, like one looking with no hope. And then I told her.

I never saw a woman so checkered in her mind. Her head was all reversed, and where had been one notion, another bobbed up to take its place, and here the other one had been previous, a new one was dancing.

"But do they do that?" she ask'. "Do they give war-crosses to *negroes*?"

"Why not?" I says. "France don't care because the fore-fathers of these soldiers were made slaves by us. She don't lay it up against *them*. That don't touch their bravery. England never has minded dark skins—look at her East Indians and Egyptians that they say are everywhere in London. Nobody cares but us. Of course France gives negroes crosses of war when they're brave—why shouldn't she?"

"My gracious," Mis' Sykes says, "but what'll folks say here if we do go ahead and recognize them?"

"Recognize *him*!" I cried. "Mis' Sykes—are you going to let him offer up his life, and go over to Europe and have his bravery recognized there, and then come back here and get the cold shoulder from you—are you? Then shame on us all!" I says.

Then Mis' Sykes said the things folks always say: "But if we recognize them, what about marriage?"

"See here," says I, "there's thousands and thousands of tuberculosis cases in this country to-day. And more hundreds of thousands with other diseases. Do we set the whole lot of them apart, and refuse to be decent to them, or do business with them, because they ought not to marry our girls and boys? Don't you see how that argument is just an excuse?"

"All the same," said Mis' Sykes, "it might happen."

"Then make a law against inter-marriage," I says. "That's easy. Nothing comes handier than making a new law. But don't snub the whole race—especially those that have risked their lives for you, Mis' Sykes!"

She stared at me, her face looking all triangular.

"It's for you to show them what to do," I pressed her. "They'll do what you do."

Mis' Sykes kind of stopped winking and breathing.

"I could make them do it, I bet you," she says, proud.

"Of course you could," I egged her on. "You could just take for granted everybody meant to be decent, and carry it off, matter-of-fact."

She stood up and walked around the room, her curl-papers setting strange on her proud ways.

"Don't figger on it, Mis' Sykes," I says. "Just think how much easier it is to be leading folks into something they ain't used to than to have them all laughing at you behind your back for getting come up with."

It wasn't the highest motive—but then, I only used it for a finishing touch. And for a tassel I says, moving off rapid:

"Now I'm going home to stir up my cake for the party."

She didn't say anything, and I went off up the street.

I remember it was one of the times when it came to me, strong, that there's something big and near working away through us, to get us to grow in spite of us. In spite of us.

And when I had my chocolate cake baked, I lay down on the lounge in my dining-room, and planned out how nice it was going to be, that night. . . .

There was a little shower, and then the sun came back again; so by the time we all began to move toward Mis' Sykes's, between seven and eight, everything was fresh and earth-smelling and wet-sweet green. And there was a lovely, flowing light, like in a dream.

Whenever I have a hard thing to do, be it house-cleaning or be it quenching down my pride, I always think of the way I see Mis' Sykes do hers. Dressed in her best gray poplin with a white lace yoke, and hair crimped front *and* back, Mis' Sykes received us all, reserved and formal—not with her real society pucker, but with her most leader-like look.

Everybody was there—nobody was lacking. There must have been above fifty. I couldn't talk for trying to reckon how each of them would act, as soon as they knew.

"Blistering Benson," says Timothy Toplady, that his wife had got him into his frock-tail coat that he keeps to be pall-bearer in, "—kind of nice to welcome in another first family, ain't it?"

Mis' Sykes heard him. "Timothy Toplady, you ain't enough democracy to shake a stick at," she says, regal; and left him squenched, but with his lips moving.

"I'm just crazy to get upstairs in the Oldmoxon House," says Mis' Hubbelthwait. "How do you s'pose they've got it furnished?"

"They're thinking more about the furniture of their heads than of their upstairs chambers," snaps back Mis' Sykes. And I see anew that whatever Mis' Sykes goes into, she goes into up to her eyes, thorough and firm.

"Calliope," she says, "you might run over now and see how they're situated. And be there with them when we come."

I knew that Mis' Sykes couldn't quite bear to make her speech with me looking at her, so I waited out in the entry and heard her do it—I couldn't help that. And honest, I think my respect for her rose while she done so, almost as much as if she'd meant what she said. Mis' Sykes is awful convincing. She can make you wish you'd worn gloves or went without, according to the way she's done herself; and so it was that night, in the cause she'd taken up with, unbeknownst.

She rapped on the table with the blue-glass paper weight.

"Friends," she says, distinct and serene, and everybody's buzzing simmered down. "Before we go over, I must tell you a little about our new—neighbors. The name as you know is Fernandez—Burton Fernandez. The father is a college professor, now in the City doing academic and scholastic work to a degree, as they say. The daughter is in one of our great universities. The mother, a graduate of a Southern college, has traveled extensive in Venice and—and otherwise. I can't believe—" here her voice wobbled just for an instant, "I can't believe that there is one here who will not understand the significance of our party when I add that the family happens to be colored. I am sure that you will agree with me—with *me*—that these elegant educations merit our approbation."

She made a little pause to let it sink in. Then she topped it off. She told them about the returned soldier and the cross of war.

"If there is anybody," said she—and I knew how she was glancing round among them; "if there is anybody who can't appreciate *that,* we'll gladly excuse them from the room."

Yes, she done it magnificent. Mis' Sykes carried the day, high-handed. I couldn't but remember, as I slipped out, how in Winter she wears ear-muffs till we've all come to consider going without them is affected.

I ran across the street, still in that golden, pouring light. In the Oldmoxon House was a surprise. Sitting with Mrs. Fernandez before the little light May fire, was her husband, and a slim, tall girl in a smoky brown dress, that was their daughter, home from her school to see her brother. Then the soldier boy came in. Even yet I can't talk much about him: A slight, silent youth, that had left his senior year at college to volunteer in the army, and had come home now to take up his life as best he could; and on the breast of his uniform shone the little cross, won by saving his white captain, under fire.

I sat with them before their hearth, but I didn't half hear what they said. I was looking at the room, and at the four quiet folks that had done so much for themselves—more than any of us in the village, in proportion—and done it on paths none of us had ever had to walk. And the things I was thinking made such a noise I couldn't pay attention to just the talk. Over and over it kept going through my head: In fifty years. *In fifty years!*

At last came the stir and shuffle I'd been waiting for and the door-bell rang.

"Don't go," they said, when I sprang up; and they followed me into the hall. So there we were when the door opened, and everybody came crowding in.

Mis' Sykes was ahead, and it came to me, when I saw how deathly pale she was, that a prejudice is a living thing, after all—not a dead thing; and that to them that are in its grasp, your heart has got to go out just as much as to them that suffer from it.

I waved my hand to them all, promiscuous, crowding in with their baskets.

"Neighbors," I says, "here's our new neighbors. Name yourselves gradual."

They set their baskets in the hall, and came into the big room where the fire was. And I was kind of nervous, because our men are no good on earth at breaking the ice, except with a pick; and our women, when they get in a strange room, are awful apt to be so taken up looking round them that they forget to work up anything to say.

But I needn't have worried. No sooner had we sat down than somebody spoke out, deep and full. Standing in the midst of us was Burton Fernandez, and it was him. And his voice went as a voice goes when it's got more to carry than just words, or just thoughts.

"My friends," he said, "I cannot bear to have you put yourselves in a false position. When you came, perhaps you didn't know. I mean—did you think, perhaps, that we were of your race?"

It was Mis' Sykes who answered him, grand and positive, and as if she was already thinking up her answer when she was born.

"Certainly not," she says. "We were informed—all of us." Then I saw her get herself together for something tremenjus, that should leave no doubt in anybody's mind. "What of that?" says she.

He stood still for a minute. He had deep-set eyes and a tired face that didn't do anything to itself when he talked. But his voice—that did. And when he began to speak again, it seemed to me that the voice of his whole race was coming through him.

"My friends," he said, "how can we talk of other things when our minds are filled with just what this means to us?"

We all kept still. None of us would have known how to say it, even if we had known what to say.

He said: "I'm not speaking of the difficulties—they don't so much matter. Nothing matters—except that even when we have made the struggle, then we're despised no less. We don't often talk to you about it—it's the surprise of this—you must forgive me. But I want you to know that from the time I began my school life, there have been many who despised, and a few who helped, but never until to-night have there been any of your people with the look and word of neighbor—never once in our lives until to-night."

In the silence that fell when he'd finished, I sat there knowing that even now it wasn't like he thought it was—and I wished that it had been so.

He put his hand on his boy's shoulder.

"It's for his sake," he said, "that I thank you most."

Mis' Sykes was equal to that, too.

"In the name of our whole town," she says to that young soldier, "we thank *you* for what you've done."

He just nodded a little, and nobody said anything more. And it came to me that most everything is more so than we most always suppose it to be.

When Mis' Toplady don't know quite what to do with a minute, she always brings her hands together in a sort of spontaneous-sounding clap, and kind of bustles her shoulders. She done that now.

"I motion I'll take charge of the refreshments," she says. "Who'll volunteer? I'm crazy to see what-all we've brought."

Everybody laughed, and rustled, easy. And I slipped over to the daughter, standing by herself by the fire-place.

"You take, don't you?" I ask' her.

"'Take?'" she says, puzzled.

"Music, I mean," I told her. (We always mean music when we say "take" in Friendship Village.)

"No," she says, "but my brother plays, sometimes."

The soldier sat down to the piano, when I asked him, and he played, soft and strong, and something beautiful. His cross shone on his breast when he moved. And me, I stood by the piano, and I heard the soul of the music come gentling through his soul, just like it didn't make any difference to the music, one way or the other. . . .

Music. Music that spoke. Music that sounded like laughing voices. . . . No, for it was laughing voices. . . .

I opened my eyes, and there in my dining-room, by the lounge, stood Mis' Toplady and Mis' Holcomb, laughing at me for being asleep. Then they sat down by me, and they didn't laugh any more.

"Calliope," Mis' Toplady says, "Mis' Sykes has been round to everybody, and told them about the Oldmoxon House folks."

"And she took a vote on what to do to-night," says Mame Holcomb.

"Giving a little advice of her own, by the wayside," Mis' Toplady adds.

I sat up and looked at them. With the soldier's music still in my ears, I couldn't take it in.

"You don't mean—" I tried to ask them.

"That's it," says Mis' Toplady. "Everybody voted to have a public meeting to honor the soldiers—the colored soldier with the rest. But that's as far as it will go."

"But he don't want to be honored!" I cried. "He wants to be neighbored—the way anybody does when they're worth it."

"Mis' Sykes says," says Mis' Toplady, "that we mustn't forget what is fitting and what isn't."

And Mis' Holcomb added: "She carried it off grand. Everybody thinks just the way she does."

My reception-surprise cake stood ready on the table. After a while, we three sat down around it, and cut it for ourselves. But all the while we ate, that soldier's music was still playing for me; and what hadn't happened was more real for me than the things that were true.

The Biography of Blade

"Born in Muscoda. Attended public school in Muscoda. Edited 'The Muscoda Republic' for twenty-five years." Blade had written his biography for the county history. He walked to his home and thought: "It's good. Not many men in the hundred millions are much better off."

He passed the house of Herron, his banker, and heard singing. A woman's voice was singing in a foreign tongue. He walked slowly and listened. In the evening sunlight the banker's house, his lawn, his bridal wreath looked luminous. The air thinned and thickened as cloud and wind wove their uneven ovals. The voice sang on. Blade felt abrupt and obscure happiness. His complacence deepened. "Pretty good. Not many men in the hundred millions are much better off."

At his home, about his table, his family gathered: the woman, all her life of Muscoda, whom he had married; their four children, contentious, smelling of toilet soap; his mother, silent and prevalent. His wife, who seemed to be dining only en route to real occupation, said:

"Mrs. Herron has asked you and mother and me to hear somebody sing there tonight. I can't go; I'm too tired." Without looking at her, Blade answered, "I'll go to the Herrons'," and his mother said that she would go. His wife, going on with her inner routine, lapsed back into speech with, "There isn't a thing in the house for breakfast."

About them countless cloudy influences surged, the melting west, the blue dusk, heightened sounds from the open. The room was a theater of airy action. Less than this were the steak, the apple pie, the general argument about the pronunciation of "slough," or, as they rose, that soft flatulence in the throat of his mother. In the redundant din of dishes, in the clamor of their voices, the faint unearthly splendor died to earthly darkness.

In the night gentle, leisurely, already experimenting with darkness, Blade and his mother went forth. The Herron lawn offered odor of sycamore and wild grape. Blade breathed it, felt happiness, and said to his mother:

"That new county history's coming out. Wonder if you'll like what it says about me." Under the porch lights the fallen muscles of her large face lifted.

In the Herrons' rooms, so regular, so inevitable, the guests gathered. The moquette, the mohair, the mahogany, received them. They were business men and their wives, the accustomed, the dutiful, the numb. There was a rote of jest, of retort, of innuendo. There were the thrilling potentialities and the deathly routine of being. All were tumultuously aware of the little fountain of life within themselves.

At their abrupt, embarrassed hush, Blade saw near the piano the Herrons' niece. Her beautiful shoulders, her body cased in blue, her slow, floating voice, invaded him. In her he saw and heard all youth, all that is luminous, all that is different. Upon

Blade invisible hands laid hold. With soft violence he was claimed, carried, torn. "What's this?" he felt, and had never felt so much. For the first time his importance, his newspaper, his home, his family, were outdistanced. He saw that this woman lived in another way than his way, and it was her way that he wanted.

At the close of her singing, he approached her. She spoke to him casually, and he thought that there must be some mistake. Could she not see that of all those in the room he it was to whom she had signaled? He felt that he was crying: "Where are you? I understand. In God's name, throw me a rope!" Instead he was saying: "You sing like a bird, Miss Herron. Much obliged, I'm sure. I—" When others intervened, he waited for a long time by the piano, the stout, smiling man. At length he found his opportunity, and said to her, "I used to play second flute myself." But he wondered whether, after all, he could have said this aloud, because she only glanced and smiled, though with that information he had sent her something vast and pleading. He did not have another chance to address her.

Out on the street his mother said, "My dinner didn't set well"; but Blade, in some powerful onslaught of the unknown, made no reply and hurried brutally.

He took a blanket and lay on the grass. There was no change in the trees or the frogs of Muscoda. There they were, true to the past. But they were new to Blade, and so were the stars. It was perhaps the seventeen-thousandth night of his life, and yet it was the first. He was feeling: "Say, music! I've always cottoned to it; but look what it *is*! Look what it *does*!" Next door a second-floor window glowed. There Edgerton, dying, lay expecting to recover. Every one knew save Edgerton. Blade had been sorry, but now he was seized and shaken by the fact that there was Edgerton, dying and not knowing. With this fact Blade quivered as occasionally, toward dawn, he had quivered with remorse or worry. He experienced Edgerton. Then he experienced delight that he himself was not dying. The pang of Miss Herron and her singing returned and returned, powerful, possessing, and at last excluding.

At daybreak he woke. Long, loose pulsations of light shook him. Was it light or was it song? He sat on his blanket and looked up from the well of his garden to the sky. He thought: "I'm going to take music lessons. I'll go and see Miss Herron to-day, talk with her about it." Countless cloudy influences surged round the lawn, where was a theater of changing light and airy action. For the first time in his life he saw the morning.

At breakfast his passion for spiritual isolation caused suspicion. "You act as if you're going to risk some more money," said his mother. "Better not." And his wife asked acutely, "What woman was there last night?" so that Blade thundered, "Can't I have quiet in my own house?" The children discreetly tittered. With a wave of nostalgia it came to Blade that by his words of thunder he had in some way cut himself off from Miss Herron. In order to get back to that world of Miss Herron, he spoke gently to his wife.

His first act at the office was to request the return of his biography copy from the editor of the county history. Blade said, "I can liven mine up a lot." It had come to him that he had written a biography which did not express his life, so rich and so potential. And now the office routine began—routine, but yet extraordinary. A pearly shadow drenched the bare room. Or was it that? You moved the radio a fraction of an inch, and you had a new wave length. Blade had a new wave length. Nothing proceeded in the old way. The men of the staff of the composing room, he saw them with incredible intensity, Johns, Lubbock, Mayhew, Platt, in their dirty ticking aprons, with rolled gold rings on the little fingers of inky hands swinging from the elbow. Had Blade ever really seen them until now? He felt in some delicious suspension; or was it balance? Exquisitely rested, he felt, and as if everything were simple. He said to one or two: "Do you know, music is a great thing. For a fact. Wish I'd kept on with second flute that time." He spoke in excitement such that, had they known of a tragedy involving Blade later in the day, they would have remembered. But they did not know of the tragedy.

At eleven o'clock he called the Herrons' house. He waited at the telephone and was rocked on the waves of expectation. A voice came: "Oh, Miss Herron? Oh, Miss Herron left this morning for her home. Who is this calling, please?" Blade mumbled: "'Muscoda Republic.' Thanks for the item." He groped to the door and stared up and down the street, but she was not passing.

He went at noon to the Muscoda Marble Counter for lunch. The place was clean, the food was good, the women who presided were perfect at their rites. Before the oil-cloth-covered counter Blade sat, and he felt the physical nausea and the shivering of a young animal at night, homeless.

And at night he stayed so long at the office, alone, that Muscoda main street was empty. At his own gate it came to him that he wanted his mother. He was glad that there was a light in her room. He tapped, and sidled toward her, intent on his nameless and infinite loss. Vast and shapeless in her red-and-black checked bath robe, she sat among her plants and bottles and regarded him without change of expression. She commented: "I thought you were going to take me to the picture show to-night." He stood stricken, not by his failure, but by hers. He mumbled and withdrew, and in the passage his wife met him, put her arms about him, whispered, "Nobody loves you as I do!" This should have surprised him, but he was not listening. His soul heard, and cried, "What of it?"

In the night he saw Edgerton's window glowing. Blade felt sorry, an impression now, not an emotion. He woke to the sun and said, "Another fine day," a formula, not a feeling. He went to his office, and the men were pale fellows, inky, disheveled, remote. He faced the blind wall of human loneliness. He was as one who, expecting to be born, is stillborn, and becomes aware not of the cradle, but of eternity.

In a few days Blade appeared before Montgomery, the Muscoda band leader, and said:

"Say, I used to play the second flute myself. And I wondered . . ."

When "one-night stands" come to Muscoda Opera House, Blade sits in the orchestra and plays the second flute. His detached wife and his grown children come to the Opera House plays, and afterward they ask him why he will deliberately make himself ridiculous by playing in the band. He does not know what to reply and takes refuge in irritability.

In the Muscoda County history Blade's biography, in fine print, stands unread in many little libraries: "Born in Muscoda. Attended public school in Muscoda. Has edited 'The Muscoda Republic' for twenty-five years." To the editor of that history Blade had returned his biography copy without change, and had said:

"I don't know what it was I was going to add. Whatever the item was, it got away from me."

The Need

"Now let's us invite in somebody," said Abel.

He looked about on the new furniture, the new piano, the two shelves of bright books.

Emily Louise clapped her hands.

"Oh," she said, "yes. Let's!"

On the face of Victoria, the mother, the pleased pride gave place to a look of trouble.

"We don't know so very many," she said.

"We!" Abel repeated. "I don't know nobody. How should I? I work all day like a dog since I came to this place. I've no time to know nobody. But you—you stay about here. Have you not made friends?"

"Not well enough to invite them in," Victoria said. "Why, you know yourself, Abel, nobody has invited us yet."

"What difference does that make?" he wanted to know irritably. "Probably they can't afford it. Probably they ain't nice enough things. Neither did we have. But now we got them. I got them for you. Now you must invite in different ones. Let us see—we have

Tuesday. Saturday is a good day. I am early home Saturday. Have it then."

"Goody, goody," said Emily Louise. "A party, won't it be?"

She went away to school. Abel ran for his train. The new things had come late in the evening and he had risen early to unpack them before he went to work. Left alone, Victoria faced the new responsibility.

They had lived for six months in the suburb. She rehearsed those to whom in that time she had spoken. There was the woman in the yellow house on the corner, to whom Victoria had once bowed, though she could not be sure that her greeting had been returned; in the brick house across the street, Mrs. Stern, who had called upon her; the next-door neighbor, who had not called, but with whom she had sometimes talked across the fence; and Emily Louise's school-teacher, Miss Moody, who had come to see her about the child's throat. With the exception of the tradespeople, these were all. How, then, was it possible that she should give a party?

But how was it that she knew no one, she wondered. It was true, they went to no church; but, then, there are people who go to no churches and who still have friends. It could not be Abel's fault—he looked just like any other man; and Emily Louise, she was a neat and pretty child. It must be she herself, Victoria thought.

She looked in the mirror of the new sideboard. She was worn and untidy. She went to her closet and examined her stock of clothes. Her black best dress, she decided, would pass very well, but she never wore it; and even her gray second-best she had seldom troubled to put on in the afternoons. It was hard to dress for nobody.

Still, that afternoon she put on the gray dress and sat rocking on the front porch for a long time. The suburb lay naked to the August sun. New sidewalks cut treeless stretches of brown grass where insects shrilled. There were few houses, and these, at ragged intervals, exposed narrow, staring fronts or backs which looked taken unawares. To and fro on the highway before her door continually rolled touring-cars, filled with people who hardly saw the little town and never knew its name. From the yellow house on the corner the woman, Mrs. Merriman, came out and crossed the street. For a moment Victoria thought that she was coming to see her, but she went to the next-door neighbor's.

"Well," said Abel that night, "I do everything I can to help you. When I got off the train, I spoke to that fine bakery place there on the corner. I told him he should make us ice-cream and make us cakes for Saturday. He says: 'Sure,' and he wants I should tell him how many."

"Abel," Victoria said, "I don't know what to do about this party. I'm not acquainted with enough folks to make a party."

"You're too particular, maybe," he told her. "Well, that is right," he added complacently, "that is how you should be, particular. But not *too.*"

"But, Abel," she persisted, "I tell you that I don't know . . ."

He turned to her indignantly.

"When I married you," he said, "you knew half the village. In Eland's you know the ladies yet. Here we have been six months already, and you say you cannot give a party. I tell you, you should ask what few you know and make a start. If you don't, how will you get started? Is it you don't appreciate what I get for you? Is it a party should make you some hard work? Or *what*?"

She was silent. That night she tried to think it out. In the morning she went to the next-door neighbor.

"My husband and I want your husband and you to come over

to our house and spend the evening next Saturday. Could you?" she recited formally.

The woman's vast face, with its unnecessary chins, was genuinely regretful. She was going that day to her mother, who was sick in the city, and her husband was to stay nights at her mother's.

Victoria went resolutely to Mrs. Stern's door, at the brick house. And there the heavens opened. Mrs. Stern would come.

"Oh, thank you!" Victoria breathed, and hesitated, deploring Mrs. Stern's widowhood. "Would—would you like to bring somebody with you?" she asked. "I'm going to have things as nice as I can."

Mrs. Stern, a sad little woman with an unexpectant droop, contrived to make her answer all kindness.

"How many can come to the party?" Abel inquired that evening.

"Mrs. Stern can come," Victoria replied.

"Well?" said Abel expectantly.

"I haven't—there isn't anyone else. Abel, I don't think I can do it, truly," she said.

The man's face tightened.

"So," he said, "you cannot do like other men's wives when they get a neat up-to-date little home furnished like this. Is that it?"

"I haven't had time yet, either, Abel," she pleaded weakly. "It takes longer. I—I haven't heard."

She remembered how hard he worked and how few were his pleasures. She thought of his pride in their new furniture. And in her flesh was the sting of his words about other men's wives. Surely he was right, since they had the furniture and the means, there must be people who would come. In the morning, when she told him good-bye in the confidence of the sun, "Abel," she said with determination, "the party will be Saturday! But I can't tell yet how many—that is the only thing."

"So," he said, his satisfaction returning. "Of course, when a person wants to give parties, people hang around them! You should manage, Victoria."

There was, Victoria knew, a little club of women which met in the parlor of a near-by public hall on Thursdays. She had seen the members pass her house on their way to the meetings. On Thursday she presented herself at the door of the little room and asked for the president. It had come to Victoria that if she could join, she would invite that whole club and their husbands to her house on Saturday evening. She waited in the ante-room, through which went women talking as if they had known each other for a long time. At last the president appeared. This woman held her head back, either to focus her glasses or to keep them on, and her hands were filled with loose papers.

"What was it?" she asked.

She was in haste, and it was hard for Victoria to begin.

"Could other folks join your club?" Victoria finally inquired.

"If you get two members of the club to propose the name," the president answered kindly. "Then it is voted on two weeks after it is proposed. Was that all?"

That night Abel came home with a large box. He was gay with mystery. The box was not to be opened until after dinner. Emily Louise was warned away. To please him Victoria guessed: a rug, a picture, new curtains, a bedspread.

"Yet more magnificent!" cried Abel, and he cut the string.

It was a suit of evening clothes. Abel had never worn evening clothes. These had been made for another man and had not been received on delivery.

"Now you should not be ashamed when I am welcoming our company," he said. "Can you tell yet how many are coming?" he demanded.

"Not yet," Victoria said.

"I should let that baker know tomorrow without fail," he declared.

On Friday Victoria took the step over which she had hesitated. She wrote a note and sent it by Emily Louise to Mrs. Merriman in the yellow house on the corner. The note said:

> MRS. MERRIMAN,
> My dear Neighbor:—
> We are going to have a party Saturday night. Will you and your husband come, and your little girl, if you think she would enjoy it. I would like to have my neighbors come.
> Yours sincerely,
> Mrs. Abel Hope

"Then," Victoria thought, "if she hasn't called just because she's been busy, she'll come."

When she was preparing lunch for herself and Emily Louise, the reply was delivered by a maid:

> Mr. and Mrs. William Merriman regret that they are unable to accept the invitation of Mr. and Mrs. Hope for Saturday evening.

Victoria dropped these regrets on the coals of the cooking-stove. Her heart was heavy in her, and she felt a kind of physical nausea. Abel had bought this fine suit. He would look like any other man giving a party and having a wife who made friends. What should she do now?

While Emily Louise ate her lunch, Victoria ate nothing. She tried to think it out, and she sat staring at the automobiles rolling on the highway. She was hardly conscious of the child's chatter until at last one sentence leaped from the rest and held her:

"Miss Moody says she's coming to see you again about my throat," said Emily Louise.

Miss Moody! Why had she not invited her?

"I like Miss Moody, but I like Mr. Allen better," Emily Louise continued candidly. "He's . . ."

Victoria bent towards the child.

"Emily Louise," she said breathlessly, "how many teachers are there in your school-house?"

At once the child became important. She named them all, proud of her knowledge, and Victoria and she counted them. There were seven.

Seven! That number in itself would make a party. People were always doing nice things for teachers. She would have them all. She said nothing to the child, but when Emily Louise returned to school, she took to Miss Moody a note asking her to invite all other teachers to Emily Louise's house for Saturday evening.

That night the child waited, as she sometimes did, for her father's train, and she came home with him. Victoria took Miss Moody's note secretly and laid it on a shelf in the pantry. She was in the midst of getting dinner, but this was not the real reason for the delay. She dreaded to open the note.

"How," Abel inquired, "is our party *now*? By now you got to know how many come. Not?"

"Ten," said Victoria faintly. "Counting us, ten."

Oh, yes, she said to herself, the teachers would come. They must come. Surely they would be glad to come.

Abel pursed his lips. "You should have got more," he rebuked her. "We could afford more, while we're doing it."

She said nothing. After dinner, while he was on the sofa playing with Emily Louise, she went to the pantry and opened the note. Miss Moody was genuinely sorry and they all were, appreciating as they did this attention from the parents of a pupil, but on Saturday night they must all be at a teachers' conference in town.

Victoria washed the dinner dishes and laid the table for breakfast. When she could make no further excuse for delay, she went in the other room to tell Abel. She was pale and faint, and when she closed the kitchen door, she stood leaning against it, trembling.

Only Emily Louise was in the room.

"Daddy's gone to the bakery to tell him how many," she announced. "Just think, mother! Tomorrow night the party'll be being! Isn't it *grand*?"

Victoria took her in her arms and sat waiting for Abel's return. She dared not think what he would do. He had a temper of unreason and of violence, and he would see only what he already saw. Yet when he came back, filled with innocent pride in the brick ice-cream and the little fancy cakes which he had selected, it was not so much her fear that held her silent as her sick unwillingness to quench that childlike planning.

"We should change the bookcase and the piano," he declared. "It will make the room stand to look wider across."

She even helped him to fold back the rug and to move the furniture.

"We should shake hands here," said he. "Where do they put their coats? Why don't you talk some planning?"

Somehow she evaded everything save assent, and Abel was not one to wonder at any monologue of his own. He arranged it all. He talked of it incessantly.

At last Victoria crept to bed and faced what on the morrow she must do. From the sleep which came to her towards dawn, she was early awakened by Emily Louise jumping in her bare feet at the bed-side and calling:

"The party's tonight! The party's tonight!"

The phrase beat at Victoria's ears through the morning. She saw Abel set off for his work, and she said to herself that she would never see him just like this again—perhaps she would never see him again at all. He would work all day thinking of the evening. They had never given a party. Then he would come home and find the truth. She confronted the chief misery of every unhappiness: the tracing of avoidable events by which the thing had so incredibly come about.

She made ready and cooked a fowl and a roast and other food, enough to last Abel for several days. She set her house in order and packed her own belongings. She put on the gray dress and dressed Emily Louise—perhaps, she thought, Abel would follow her for the sake of the child, and then she might make him understand. After their lunch she sat down to write two notes. The one to Mrs. Stern was brief and explained that she had been obliged unexpectedly to leave home. The note to Abel was harder to write.

> DEAR ABEL:—I am so sorry it will hurt you that I couldn't invite a party like the other women. I tried to. I asked the ones I know any, but only Mrs. Stern could, and anyway there wasn't enough. . . .

She was still writing at this when she heard a sharp noise and voices. In the road was standing a motor car. She watched the men descend and examine the machine, and then one of them came to her door. Victoria had never spoken with a man like him or heard speech so perfect. When she had told him that she had no telephone and had directed him to Mrs. Stern's house, she could not forbear a sympathetic question.

"Thank you, yes," he said. "A rear axle. If it had been a front one . . ."

He smiled, and Victoria smiled too, although to her his words meant nothing.

"We'll be tied up for some time, I'm afraid," he added.

There were in the car three women and three men. Presently Victoria saw them all go into Mrs. Stern's garden. One of the women had to be helped a little. She went into the house, but the others sat under the trees.

Mrs. Stern came running across the street.

"Oh, Mrs. Hope," she said, her dull face quickened, "have you any lemons in the house? Those folks have got to sit here till they can send out someone from the city to mend their car—one of the ladies is lame. I thought I'd give them something cool to drink."

Victoria was looking at her breathlessly.

"Do you think," she said, "that they'd come over here with you for dinner? I could have it real prompt."

To the Audreys and their friends, sitting somewhat disconsolately in Mrs. Stern's little garden, Victoria appeared in a confusion that unmasked her eagerness. They protested: it was too much; their own dinner hour was late—there was no need. . . .

"I want you should come," Victoria said earnestly, as if there were a need. "I never have any company out here. I want you to come."

They followed her involuntary glance to the treeless stretches and the sidewalks that led nowhere and that betrayed to how few footsteps they ever echoed. Some hint of Victoria's tragedy was in the bleak open of the blocks.

"Why, thank you," Mrs. Audrey said gently. "Then if you will really let us, we will come."

Victoria could hardly believe. She sped across the street, the past days fallen from her. She made ready the roast and the fowl that she had meant to leave for Abel, the vegetables and salad fresh from the garden. Emily Louise was sent to hurry the baker, and later to strip the vines of their sweet peas. Many tasks were to be done, but Victoria made of them nothing. When Abel came home, the savor of the preparation filled the little house.

"It's a dinner!" she triumphantly told him.

"A dinner! So that was what was up your sleeve!" cried Abel, and he ran to look over the table. "That is right—that is fine," he approved, "only we should had more here. It was no more trouble—to have more."

At six o'clock all was ready: Victoria in her black best gown, Abel in the new suit, of which the sleeves were a bit too long, so that he constantly pushed them up at the armholes. When he saw their guests at the gate, he drew Victoria to the place he had appointed. Emily Louise opened the door.

"Most pleased to welcome you hospitable under my little roof," Abel said, as he had planned to say.

He mastered the names by careful attention and repetition. Victoria slipped away to serve the dinner. When she called them with: "You can come now," from the doorway, Abel genially led the way.

"Take your seats where you like!" he cried.

The six guests were from another world. Of everything that they did they made graces. At Abel's table they were instantly at home, and they were found putting Victoria at her ease.

"You in business around here or in the city?" Abel inquired of Audrey.

Audrey, a man of forty, of fine distinction and fine humor and a genuine love of men replied that his work was in town.

"What company you with?" Abel wished to know. "The Badington Electric!" he repeated with a shout. "Why, that's my firm! Sure—I'm for ten years a builder. What's your job with them, may I ask? Travel for them, maybe?"

"Something of that sort," said Audrey, to whom a major part of the Badington Electric belonged. "All three of us here are slaves for that company," he added.

"Well, then," cried Abel, "we are already acquainted, ain't it? We understand each other like a family. We got a kind of a common feeling. Not?"

After that the talk made itself. Abel talked, and to his eyes came the passion of the men with whom he worked, their needs, their bonds, their confusions. The three men listened and said what they could, wondering at this unfamiliar agglomeration which to Abel meant the firm; and then they sought to show him vistas of which he had taken no account. The guests praised the little house, and Victoria told them how, though she herself had lived in a village and had had more experience, until now Abel had always lived in a flat. "Abel's never lived before, what you might say, private," she said.

When the brick ice-cream and the baker's little cakes were set before them, Abel kept silence while he ate, as one giving meet observance; and he sent glances of pleased pride to Victoria.

Finally Abel proposed to the men that they go out to the porch, "where we can smoke," and the women, who had fallen in talk about Emily Louise, were left lingering at the table. Mrs. Audrey had a little girl at home, the others had children grown. The three women told anecdotes of childish doings.

"Your little girl must be a great deal of company for you," the lame lady said quaintly.

"She has to be," Victoria said. And in the warmth of their presence, she told them the history of her party and of how it had almost failed. The furniture, the club, her other invitations—she told it all; but Abel's new suit she did not mention.

"Well, now," said Abel, when they went with their guests to their car, "you must all drop in on us some evening. We'd like it, wouldn't we, Victoria?"

"We mean to come," the women told Victoria.

"And I'll look you up at the works some time, if you don't mind," Audrey heard himself saying to Abel.

"Sure," said Abel, "we stand to know each other better from now on—not? That is what a man needs. Sure!"

"Come soon again—come soon again!" Emily Louise called after the car.

Mrs. Stern was speaking to Victoria.

"That club you told us about," she said, "I belong to that. I'll get your name put up, if you would like that."

Having carefully changed the new suit, Abel went into the kitchen to help his wife with the dishes and to talk it over. To his surprise, she had done nothing; she stood leaning in the outside kitchen doorway. In the late light the open land had almost the face of the country; and to that which had seemed to be defined, color of twilight was now giving new depths and delicacies. He came and stood beside her.

"Victoria," he said admiringly, "where'd you meet them? They're the right kind of friends for anybody!"

Then she told him, in her happiness and her contrition. And she showed him the note that she had meant to leave. For an instant something of her tragedy was clear to Abel. He put out his hand.

"I don't care how you done it," he said loyally, "you done it magnificent."

Bridal Pond

The Judge had just said "Case dismissed," and a sharp situation concerning cheese had thus become negligible when, before the next case on the calendar could be called, Jens Jevins came forward and said loudly:

"I wish to confess to the murder of my wife."

Now the court-room was still, the fierce heat forgotten and the people stupefied, for Jens Jevins was the richest farmer in the township. No one tried to silence or delay him.

He faced now the Judge and now the people, his face and neck the color of chicken skin, his tossed hair like a raveled fabric, his long right arm making always the same gesture. His clothes were good, and someone had pressed them.

"I planned to kill Agna for a long time. There was a time when for a week I slept with a pistol under my pillow, hoping for the strength to shoot her in her sleep. When I could tell by her breathing that it was time, I'd get up on my elbow and look at her, but I never had the courage to use the pistol on her—no, though I sat up in bed sometimes for half an hour with my finger on the trigger. Something would delay me—our dog would bark, or the kitchen clock would strike, or I would imagine my father shaking his head at me; and once she woke and asked me whether I had locked the porch door.

"Most of that week the room was as bright as morning, because the moon shone in, but as it rose later and hung higher, the room grew dark. And it seemed wrong to shoot Agna in the dark. Then I thought of a better plan."

The court-room was held as a ball of glass, in which black figures hang in arrested motion. The silence was not vacant, but rich and winy, like a rest in music. It was the rest in the tread of a giant, one step, one step, and men crushed and powerless. The Judge, the bailiff, the spectators were crushed and powerless, all with staring eyes, and their short breath caught through the mouth. Jens and Agna Jevins, they were known to all, and he so prosperous; and she a small complaining woman, who took prizes, with whom all must have talked on bright mornings, after she had lain asleep, close to death.

"At the south of our lot," Jens Jevins continued, and conversationally, quite quietly, as if he were talking to some surveyors, "there is a long slope and then a pond, where in my father's time they took out clay to make bricks. This place is not fenced; is separated from the highway by a few alders—some of you know," he said, with an air of surprise, remembering the spectators as living beings who had experienced his highway and the sight of his pond. "I would go down there sometimes on spring evenings when the boys were catching frogs, and last week I went down, and they were catching frogs. And it was the night the Alexander boy fell in—well over his head he went, for the pond is above seven feet deep there, and sixteen farther out. I, that was standing near, was able to seize on him—I mention this because pulling him out put in my head the idea of what to do to Agna.

"So the next night I waited till late, and I said to her that we might walk down and watch the boys catch frogs. She was glad to go and mentioned that I didn't often invite her to take evening walks any more, and we went down the slope. But I hadn't waited long enough, the boys were still there. She and I stood on the rim of the pond, and I edged her towards the place where the Alexander boy went in, and saw how easy it would be to send her down and keep her from climbing out. Only the boys were still there.

"It was dusk, and the cars from town came down the highway and took the turn beyond our alders, and it looked as if they were all coming straight on to us, till they swung the corner. She says: 'What if one didn't see the turn and came crashing on to us?' and she shivered and said her shoulders were chilly, though the night was warm, and she wanted to go back to the house. So we went back and I read the evening paper aloud, about a young couple that had got married that day at Sun Prairie and had had a great doings. She said she wished we were starting over, and I said: 'I don't' and went to bed.

"But in the night I woke up and thought of what she'd said. What if we were starting over? And what if I'd murdered her early—say, on the honeymoon? I saw that I couldn't have done it then. I wondered how I could do it now."

Now the Judge found his voice, and leaned down as if he were ill or drunk, and said from his throat: "Why did you want to do it?"

Jens Jevins looked astonished. "I didn't *want* to do it," he said, "but there was thirty-seven years of it already and there might be twenty more."

Having answered, he continued:

"I began to see that what wasn't tragedy now would have been tragedy then. I thought of us driving through the country, if we'd been in the days of machines, like the Sun Prairie couple. Agna and me, you understand—and her young again. Her in the same blue dress, in the seat beside me. Me in a new suit, and shoes with the new not off the soles. Us talking and laughing, our valises stowed in the back. Going along the road. Along the road that swung round by our place and turned the corner by the alder-trees. Dark it might be, or maybe a fog would have come down. We'd be talking and laughing, and the road strange, and I'd miss the turn, and the car'd come skimming between the alders and across the base of the slope and making for the clay hole. Spite of all I could do, setting the brakes, on it'd come, heading for the clay hole. In the dark or maybe in the fog. And we wouldn't know we'd left the road till I'd see a light from somewhere lapping on the pond, and then it'd be too late. Straight in and down—in and down. Nothing I could do. Agna in her blue dress. On the day of our wedding.

"But now it was thirty years and past, and twenty more to come. I woke her up. I says: 'I can't sleep. It's warm. Let's go down and walk out somewheres.' She laughed and grumbled some, but she went with me. She was always one to go with me. We put on little and went down the slope to the pond. It was deep dark—the light of a star was deep in the water. We heard the frogs and smelled the first wild grape. I took her to the place where the Alexander boy had slipped in and where it was hard for anybody to climb out. I waited a minute. Another car was coming along the road. 'When it turns the corner,' I thought, 'when it turns!' Its lights shone straight and strong, they blinded us, they came on and on, towards us. Agna says: 'It's coming, it's coming! . . .' For the lights made no turn at the corner. The lights shot out from the alders. I could hear the talking and laughing in the car. In less than a flash of time the car shook the ground around us and went crashing down and down into the deep of the water. But first the lights of the water, or of the dashboard, or of the sky, or of heaven struck full on their faces, that were still laughing. Well, there on that seat, I tell you, I saw me in my wedding-suit, that was new, and beside me Agna, that was young again.

"There was a cry from Agna, that was young, and from me where I stood—and I saw what I'd done—reached back into the past and killed her that it was tragedy to kill. It was so that it had found me out. God had done it to me—just that way. I see it so. . . . All night I've walked in the woods, waiting for the time to tell. Now you know—now you know."

Jens Jevins stood, head down, abruptly distracted, listless. The hundred voices in the room burst their silence. And after the first words, crude and broken, the women were saying: "Walked all night in the woods? But somebody has just pressed his clothes for him!"

Now the sound of running feet and the cries of men reached the room, and as these increased, none knew whether to run down into the street or to stay in the court-room, where Jens Jevins might say something more. But now a great gasping voice cried from the stair: "Car gone into Jevins's clay hole!". . . and immediately the room was emptied of all but those who must stay, and Jevins, who seemed not to have heard.

As one man, and he breathing his horror, the town of Tarnham ran down the highway and did not take the turn, but kept straight on and flowed over the green and spangled slope and surrounded the Jevins pond. Some highway men, placing signs, had seen the corner of a top protruding from the water.

And now policemen and firemen were lifting from the water, slowly and with sickening lurchings and saggings, a black coupé, new by the signs, and within it the seated figures of man and woman. And all about them, on sides and back of the car, were gay ribbon streamers, white and pink, and lettering said: "Yes, we're just married." And such signs were also pasted on paper, and from the car was dangling a water-soaked old shoe. A young chap he was, with his hands still on the wheel, and the emergency brake set, and a rose on his coat lapel; and his young bride, in her neat gown of blue, had her hands folded in her lap, over a little silver bag.

Now the sheriff came leading Jens Jevins and pushed through the crowd, and the people moved respectfully, for the tale of the court-room had not yet gone about. The sheriff and Jen Jevins went to the two figures, taken from the car and covered on the grass, and Jens said in a loud voice: "There we are!" And now he shouted in agony, "Agna, Agna! Jens!" and cast himself on the ground beside the two still figures.

The people were stupefied, not knowing what to feel, with the men and women from the court-room murmuring his story. Jens Jevins—and he so prosperous and known to them all! They had seen him yesterday, buying and selling. Could his wife have been in the car, too—the complaining woman, who took prizes?

No, for here she came walking down the slope from the house, wondering at the crowd gathered about their pond. She looked questioning, in her neat black dress and her striped scarf, and they made way for her; and a neighbor who had been in the court-room cried: "Mrs. Jevins, Mrs. Jevins! The car that you saw last night go into the water had a bride and groom!"

But Agna Jevins said: "What car? I saw no car go into the water."

"What! You were not out here in the night and saw this car. . . ?"

"I?" cried Agna Jevins. "I was in bed the whole night, and Jens too. What car . . ."

They told her. She covered her eyes and said: "God forgive me, I heard a cry and thought of saying so to Jens, but he was sleeping soundly."

Jens and the sheriff moved toward her, and when he came up to her, Jens began speaking softly: "All our friends, Agna, thinking of us through the night. And who could have imagined that we were spending the whole night so, side by side; and with the sunrise, we still so near to each other, saying nothing. Who could have told us in our early youth: 'You will rest on that night in a bed of ooze, and none shall know or care that you lie passionless and forgotten'? Who could have known that our wedding-day and our death night would be one, because of a pond beyond alders, pleasant and secured? We have died with our dream and our happiness upon us; neither trouble nor weariness has touched us, nor the slow rust of unending days. I have no need to send you to your death, for we have died in the safety of our youth and not in the deep of days already dead. . . ."

They led him to his house.

Weeping, Mrs. Jevins said: "It must have come on him all of a rush. For I pressed his clothes and got his breakfast and he went out of the house. And nothing had changed."

The legend grew that Jens Jevins had had a vision of that happening of the night, and that it had sent him off his head.

This book is for
Constance Ayers Denne and Clarence J. Denne, Jr.
and
Roger, Jane, and Claire Panetta

ACKNOWLEDGMENTS

We would like to express our appreciation to Joseph Balducci and Ed Helmrich of the Arrigoni and Ryan Libraries at Iona College for their work in locating Zona Gale materials. It heartens us that many individuals are advancing the reputation and readership of Zona Gale, including Nancy Breitsprecher of Fort Atkinson, Wisconsin; Judy Eulberg of Portage High School in Wisconsin; Blanche Murtagh, project director for over a decade of *Friendship Village Celebrates Zona Gale* (a daylong series of events held annually in Portage on the third Saturday in August); and Deborah Williams of the Department of English at Iona College.

Three works have been especially important sources of information and insight: August Derleth's *Still Small Voice: The Biography of Zona Gale* (1940), Harold P. Simonson's *Zona Gale* (1962), and Julia C. Ehrhardt's *Writers of Conviction* (2004).